Growing up near the beach, **Annie West** spent lots of time observing tall, burnished lifeguards—early research! Now she spends her days fantasising about gorgeous men and their love lives. Annie has been a reader all her life. She also loves travel, long walks, good company and great food. You can contact her at annie@annie-west.com or via PO Box 1041, Warners Bay, NSW 2282, Australia.

WEDDING NIGHT REUNION IN GREECE

ANNIE WEST

MILLS & BOON

First Published in Great Britain 2019
by Mills & Boon, an imprint of HarperCollins*Publishers*
1 London Bridge Street, London, SE1 9GF

© 2019 Annie West

ISBN: 978-0-263-27060-0

MIX
Paper from
responsible sources
FSC www.fsc.org   FSC® C007454

This book is produced from independently certified FSC™ paper
to ensure responsible forest management.
For more information visit www.harpercollins.co.uk/green.

Printed and bound in Spain
by CPI, Barcelona

Dedicated with thanks and affection to the people of Corfu, whose warmth made my first visit to that beautiful island so memorable.

CHAPTER ONE

'CONGRATULATIONS, CHRISTO.' DAMEN grinned and gripped his friend's arm in a hard clasp. 'I didn't think I'd ever see the day.'

'You didn't think I'd invite you to my wedding?' Christo smiled. Who else would he ask to stand up as his best man but Damen, his friend since childhood?

'You know what I mean. I never expected to see you married till you'd played the field for another decade and decided it was time to breed some heirs.'

The look that passed between them revealed their shared understanding of what it meant to be the sole male heir to a family dynasty—Damen's in shipping and Christo's in property. There were expectations and responsibilities, always, even if they came with the cushion of wealth and privilege.

At the thought of his newest responsibility, Christo rolled his shoulders. The stiffness pinching the back of his neck was familiar. But now he could relax. With the wedding over, his plans fell into place. He'd had a problem and he'd fixed it, simple as that. Life could resume its even course. The glow of satisfaction he'd felt as he'd slid the ring onto Emma's small hand burned brighter.

Everything had worked out perfectly.

'I'm glad you could get here at short notice.' Despite Christo's lack of sentimentality, it felt good to have his old friend with him.

Besides, it would have looked strange if there'd been no one from the groom's side, even at such a small wedding. Damen had arrived in Melbourne just in time for the private ceremony. Now, in the gardens of the bride's home, this was their first opportunity to talk.

'She's not what I expected, your little bride.'

Christo raised an enquiring eyebrow.

'She's besotted with you for a start. What she sees in you...' Damen shook his head in mock puzzlement, as if women didn't swarm around Christo like bees around blossom. It was another thing they had in common.

'Of course Emma's besotted. She's marrying *me*.'

Christo had no false modesty about his appeal to the opposite sex. Besides, he'd wooed old Katsoyiannis's granddaughter carefully, taking his time in a way that wasn't usually necessary to win a woman. Having his proposal rejected hadn't figured in Christo's plans.

He'd done an excellent job. A spark of heat ignited at the memory of Emma's wide-eyed gaze and the eager way she'd returned his perfunctory end-of-ceremony kiss, tempting him to prolong it into something more passionate. Christo's hands had tightened on her slender waist and he'd found himself looking forward to tonight when he'd take her to his bed for the first time.

Damen huffed out a laugh. 'There speaks the mighty Christo Karides, ego as big as the Mediterranean.' He frowned and glanced back at the house, as if confirming they were alone. Everyone was at the wedding breakfast on the far side of the building. 'But, seriously, I was surprised. Emma's lovely. Very sweet.' Another pause. 'But not your usual type.' His look turned piercing. 'I'd have thought her cousin more your speed. The vivacious redhead.'

Christo nodded, picturing Maia's pin-up-perfect curves in the tight clothes she favoured. Her confidence, her sexy banter as she'd tried to hook his attention. She would have succeeded, too, if things had been different.

A twinge of pain seared from Christo's skull to his shoulders and he rubbed a hand around his neck.

'You're right, she's gorgeous. In other circumstances we'd have had fun together.' He shook his head. His situation was immutable. Regrets were useless. 'But this is marriage we're talking about, not pleasure.'

A muffled sound made Christo turn to scrutinise the back of the large house. But there was no movement at the windows, no one on the flagstone patio or sweeping lawn. No sound except the distant strains of music.

He'd have to return to the celebration soon before his bride wondered what was taking him so long.

A beat of satisfaction quickened Christo's pulse. 'Emma's not sexy and sophisticated like her cousin, or as beautiful, but her grandfather left her the Athens property I came to buy. Marriage was the price of acquiring it.'

Damen's smile faded. 'You married for *that*? I knew the deal was important but surely you didn't need to—?'

'You're right. Normally I wouldn't consider it, but circumstances changed.' Christo shrugged and adopted a nonchalant expression to camouflage the tension he still felt at the profound changes in his life. 'I find myself in the bizarre situation of inheriting responsibility for a child.' Saying it aloud didn't make it sound any more palatable, or lessen his lingering shock. 'Can you imagine *me* as a father?'

He nodded as his friend's eyes bulged. 'You see why marriage suddenly became necessary, if not appealing. It isn't a sexy siren I need. Instead I've acquired a gentle, sensible homebody who wants only to please me. She'll make the perfect caring mother.'

Emma's hands gripped the edge of the basin so tight, she couldn't feel her fingers. That was one small mercy because the rest of her felt like one huge, raw wound throbbing in acute agony.

She blinked and stared at the mirror in the downstairs rear bathroom. The one to which she and her bridesmaid had retired for a quick make-up fix as the bathroom at the front of the house was engaged. The one with an open window, obscured by ivy, that gave onto the sprawling back garden.

In the mirror, dazed hazel eyes stared back at her. Her mouth in that new lipstick she'd thought so sophisticated was a crumpled line of colour too bright for parchment-pale cheeks.

Around her white face she still wore the antique lace of her grandmother's veil.

Emma shuddered and shut her eyes, suddenly hating the weight of the lace against her cheeks and the long wedding dress around her shaky legs. The fitted gown, so perfect before, now clasped her too tightly, making her skin clammy, nipping at her waist and breasts and squeezing her lungs till she thought they might burst.

'Did you know?'

Emma's eyes popped open to meet Steph's in the mirror. Instead of turning into a wax doll like Emma, shock made Steph look vibrant. Her eyes sparked and a flush climbed her cheeks.

'Stupid question. Of course you didn't know.' Her friend's generous mouth twisted into a snarl. 'I'll kill him with my bare hands. No, killing's too good. Slow torture. That's what he deserves.' She scowled ferociously. 'How could he treat you that way? He must know how you feel about him.'

The pain in Emma's chest intensified from terrible to excruciating. It felt as though she was being torn apart. Which made sense, as she'd been foolish enough to hand her heart to Christo Karides and he'd just ripped it out.

Without warning.

Without anaesthetic.

Without apology.

'Because he doesn't care.' The words slipped through numb lips. 'He never really cared about me.'

As soon as she said the words aloud Emma felt their truth, despite the romantic spell Christo had woven around her. He'd been kind and understanding, tender and support-ive, as she'd grappled with her grandfather's death. She'd taken his old-fashioned courtesy as proof of his respect for her, his willingness to wait. Now she realised his patience and restraint had been because he didn't fancy her at all.

Nausea surged as the blindfold ripped from her eyes.

Why hadn't she seen it before? Why hadn't she listened to Steph when she'd spoken of taking things slowly? Of not making important decisions while she was emotion-ally vulnerable?

Emma had been lost in a fairy tale this last month, a fairy tale where, as grief struck yet again, her Prince Charming was with her, not to rescue her but to be there for her, making her feel she wasn't alone.

Everyone she'd loved in this life had died. Her parents when she was eleven, abruptly wiped out of her life when the small plane they'd been in went down in a storm. Then her grandmother four years ago when Emma was eighteen. And now her opinionated, hopelessly old-fashioned yet wonderful Papou. The sense of loss had been unbearable, except when Christo had been beside her.

She drew a sharp breath that lanced tight lungs, then let it out on a bitter laugh. 'He doesn't even know who I am. He has no idea.'

Wants only to please him, indeed!

A homebody!

Obviously Christo had believed Papou, who'd insisted on thinking she studied to fill in time before she found the right man to marry!

Maybe Christo thought she lived in her grandparents' house because she was meek and obedient. The truth was that, despite his bluster, Papou had been lost when her grandmother had died and Emma had decided to stay till he recovered. But then his health had failed and there'd been no good time to leave.

The tragedy of it was that Emma had thought Christo truly understood her. She'd believed he spent time with her because he found her interesting and attractive.

But not as attractive as her *vivacious, gorgeous* cousin Maia.

Pain cramped Emma's belly and her breath sawed from constricted lungs.

Bad enough that Christo viewed her as a plain Jane compared with her *sexy siren* cousin. But the fact he hadn't noticed that Maia was warm-hearted, intelligent and funny, as well as sexy, somehow made it worse.

Christo was a clever man. According to Papou, his insightfulness had made him phenomenally successful, transforming the family business he'd inherited. Clearly Christo didn't waste time applying that insight to the women he met.

Because we're not important enough?

Because he thinks we're simply available for him to use as he sees fit?

What that said about his attitude to women made Emma's skin shrink against her bones.

He had a reputation as a playboy in Europe, always dating impossibly glamorous, gorgeous women. But in her naivety Emma had dismissed the media gossip. She'd believed him when he'd assured her his reputation was exaggerated. Then he'd stroked her cheek, his hand dropping to her collarbone, tracing the decorous neckline of her dress, and Emma had forgotten her doubts and her train of thought.

She'd been so easy to manipulate! Ready to fall for his practised charm. For his attentiveness.

Because he was the first man who'd really noticed her.

Was she really so easily conned?

Emma lurched forward over the basin as nausea rocketed up from her stomach. Bile burnt the back of her throat and she retched again and again.

When it was over, and she'd rinsed her mouth and face, she looked up at her friend. 'I *believed* in him, Steph. I actually thought the fact he didn't respond to Maia was proof he was genuinely attracted to *me*.' Her voice rose to something like a wail and Emma bit her lip.

She'd been gullible. She'd brushed aside her friend's tentative questions about the speed of Christo's courtship. At the time it had made sense to marry quickly so her Papou could be with them. And when he'd died, well, the last thing he'd said to her was how happy he was knowing she had Christo and that he didn't want her to delay the wedding.

She should have waited.

She should have known romantic fantasies were too good to be true.

'I've been a complete idiot, haven't I?' She'd always been careful—cautious rather than adventurous, sensible rather than impulsive—yet she'd let a handsome face and a lying, cheating, silver tongue distract her from her career plans and her innate caution.

'Of course not, sweetie.' Steph put her arm around her shoulders, squeezing tight. 'You're warm and generous and honest and you always look for the good in people.'

Emma shook her head, dredging up a tight smile at her friend's loyalty. 'You mean I usually have my head in the sand.' Or in books. Papou had regularly complained that she spent too much time with her nose in a book. 'Well, not any more.' She shuddered as ice frosted her spine. 'Imagine if we hadn't heard…'

'But we did.' Steph squeezed her shoulder again. 'The question is, what are you going to do about it?'

The question jolted her out of self-pity.

Emma looked in the mirror, taking in the ashen-faced waif dressed in wedding lace. Suddenly, in a burst of glorious heat, anger swamped her. Scorching, fiery anger that ran along her veins, licking warmth back into her cold flesh and burning away the vulnerability she'd felt at Christo's casual contempt. The flush of it rose from her belly to her breasts and up to her cheeks as she swung round to face her friend.

'Walk away, of course. Christo can find another *sensible* woman to care for his child and please him.'

Silly that, of all the assumptions he'd made about her and the games he'd played, what rankled most was that he'd recognised her longing for physical pleasure. For *him*.

A shudder ran through her at the thought of how she'd looked forward to pleasing him and having him reciprocate with those big, supple hands and that hard, masculine body.

Now the idea of him touching her made her feel sick.

Especially as the reason he'd abstained from sex clearly hadn't been out of respect for her and for her dying grandfather. It had been because sex with the dowdy mouse of the family hadn't appealed to him. If Christo had been engaged to the beautiful Maia, there'd have been no holding back. They'd have been scorching the sheets well before the wedding.

A curl of flame branded deep inside Emma's feminine core. In the place where, one day, a man she loved and who loved her back would possess her. She'd thought she'd found him in Christo Karides. Now all she felt was loathing for him and disappointment at herself for believing his lies.

'I'm so relieved.' Steph's words tugged her into the present. 'I was afraid you might think of staying with him and hoping he'd eventually fall in love with you.'

Emma shook her head, the old lace swishing around her shoulders. Papou had been proud that she'd wear the same veil his bride had worn to her wedding. This marriage had meant so much to him. But it was a sham. Christo hadn't only made a fool of her but of her grandfather too. She'd never forgive him that.

'I might be the quiet one in the family but I'm not a doormat. As Christo Karides is about to find out.' She met her friend's eyes in the mirror. 'Will you help me?'

'You have to ask?' Steph rolled her eyes. 'What do you have in mind?'

Emma hesitated, realising she had nothing in mind. But only for a second.

'Can you go up to my room and grab my passport and bag? And my suitcase?' The case she'd packed for her honeymoon. The thought was a jab to her heart. She sucked in a fortifying breath. 'You'll have to come down the back stairs.'

'Then what?'

'I'll book a flight out of here. If I can borrow your car and leave it at the airport—'

'And leave Christo Karides to face the music when his bride disappears? I love it.' Steph's grin almost hid the fury glittering in her eyes. 'But I've got a better idea. Forget the airport. That's the first place he'll look. With his resources, he'll be on your trail within hours. Head to my place and wait for a call.' She reached into her purse and pulled out her key ring, pressing it into Emma's hand. 'I'll get you out of Melbourne but so he can't trace your movements. I'm not the best travel agent in the city for nothing. It's going to be a real pleasure watching him stew when he can't find you.'

For the first time since overhearing Christo's conversation, Emma smiled. It didn't matter that her cheeks felt so taut they might crack, or that the pain in her heart was as deep as ever. What mattered was that she had a way out and a true friend.

Suddenly she didn't feel so appallingly alone and vulnerable.

'Thank you, Steph. I can't tell you what it means to have your help.' Emma blinked against the self-pitying tears prickling the back of her eyes.

She'd cried when she'd lost Papou. She refused to shed tears over a man who wasn't fit to speak her grandfather's name. A schemer who'd played upon the old man's love and fear for his granddaughter's future.

'But you'll have to be careful not to give me away.' Emma frowned at her friend. 'One look at your face and Christo will know you're hiding something. He may be a louse but he's smart.'

Silly how speaking of him like that sent a fillip of pleasure through her. It was a tiny thing compared with the wrong he'd done her, but it was a start.

Steph shook her head and put on the butter-wouldn't-melt-in-her-mouth expression that had fooled their teachers for years. 'Don't worry. He won't suspect a thing. I'll tell him you need a short rest. He'll accept that. He knows this has been a whirlwind, plus you're missing your grandfather.'

Steph's words sent a shaft of longing through Emma for the old man who'd been bossy and difficult but always loving beneath his gruff exterior. She blinked, refusing to give in to grief now.

'Great. You go upstairs while I get this veil off.' There was no time to get out of the dress, but she couldn't make her escape in trailing lace. 'I'll hide it in the cupboard here, if you can collect it later and look after it for me?'

'Of course. I know it's precious.' Steph put her hand on Emma's arm, squeezing gently. 'Just one more thing. Where are you travelling to?'

Emma turned to the mirror and started searching for the multitude of pins that secured the veil. 'The only place that's still home.' Her aunt and uncle, Maia's parents, had inherited this house and Papou's Australian assets. She'd got the commercial property in Athens that had then been signed over to her husband to manage. She'd have to do something about that, she realised. Plus, she'd inherited her grandparents' old villa in Greece. The one where she'd gone each year on holiday with her parents till they'd died. 'I'm going to Corfu.'

It was the perfect bolthole. She'd never mentioned it to Christo and, anyway, he would never look for her on his home turf of Greece.

She could take her time there, deciding what she planned to do. And how she'd end this farce of a marriage.

CHAPTER TWO

EMMA STEPPED THROUGH the wrought-iron gates and felt the past wash over her. She hadn't been to Corfu for years, not since she was fifteen, when her grandmother had grown too frail for long-distance travel.

Seven years, yet it felt more like seven days as she took in the shaded avenue ahead curling towards the villa just out of sight. Ancient olive trees, their bodies twisted but their boughs healthy with new growth, drifted down the slope to the sea like a silvery green blanket. Nearby glossy citrus leaves clustered around creamy buds in the orchard.

Emma inhaled the rich scent of blossom from lemon, kumquat and orange trees. Her lips tightened. Orange blossom was traditional for brides. It had been in short supply in Melbourne during autumn, unlike Greece in spring.

She shivered as something dark and chilly skipped down her spine.

What a close shave she'd had. Imagine if she hadn't learned of Christo's real agenda! She cringed to think how much further under his spell she'd have fallen. Given his reputation, she had no doubt his skills at seduction were as excellent as his ability to feign attraction.

Swallowing down the writhing knot of hurt in her throat, she grabbed the handle of her suitcase, hitched her shoulder bag higher and set off towards the house.

She was sticky and tired and longing for a cold drink. Silly of her, perhaps, to have the taxi drop her further down the road, near a cluster of new luxury villas that had sprung up in the last few years. But she didn't want to take the chance of anyone knowing she was staying here, in case word somehow got back to Christo.

She'd confront him in her own time, not his. For now she needed to regroup and lick her wounds.

Emma trudged down the drive, the crunch of her feet and her suitcase wheels on the gravel loud in the quiet. Yet, as she walked, her steps grew lighter as memories crowded close. Happy memories, for it was here her family had gathered year after year for a month's vacation.

Drops of bright colour in the olive grove caught her eye and she remembered picking wildflowers there, plonking them in her grandmother's priceless crystal vases, where they'd be displayed as proudly as if they were professional floral arrangements. Swimming with her parents down in the clear green waters of their private cove. Sitting under the shade of the colonnade that ran around three sides of the courtyard while Papou had taught her to play *tavli*, clicking the counters around the board so quickly his hand seemed to blur before her eyes.

They were gone now, all of them.

Emma stumbled to a halt, pain shearing through her middle, transfixing her.

She took a deep breath and forced herself to walk on. Yes, they'd died, but they'd taught her the value of living life to the full, and of love. Even now she felt that love as if the old estate that had been in Papou's family for years wrapped her in its embrace.

Rounding the curve in the long drive, she caught sight of the villa. It showed its age, like a gracious old lady, still elegant despite the years. Its walls were a muted tone between blush-pink and palest orange that glowed softly in the afternoon light. The tall wooden window shutters gleamed with new forest-green paint but the ancient roof tiles had weathered to a grey that looked as ancient as the stone walls edging the olive grove. Despite being a couple of hundred years old, the place was well-maintained. Papou wouldn't have had it any other way.

Nor would Emma. She was its owner now. She stood, looking at the fine old house and feeling a swell of pride and belonging she'd never felt for her grandparents' Melbourne place. This was the home of her heart, she realised. With precious memories of her parents.

A tickle of an idea began to form in her tired brain. Maybe, just maybe, this could be more than a temporary refuge before she returned to Australia. Perhaps…

Her thoughts trailed off as the front door opened and a woman appeared, lifting her hand to shade her face.

'Miss Emma?'

The familiar sound of Dora Panayiotis's heavy accent peeled the years right back. Suddenly Emma was a scrawny kid again. She left her bag and hurried forward into sturdy, welcoming arms.

'Dora!' She hugged the housekeeper back, her exhaustion forgotten. 'It's so good to see you.'

'And you, Miss Emma. Welcome home.'

Emma flicked her sodden hair off her face as she reached for the towel, rubbing briskly till her skin tingled. Early rain had cleared to a sparkling bright afternoon and she hadn't been able to resist the lure of the white sand cove at the bottom of the garden. Turquoise shallows gave way to teal-green depths that enticed far more than the pool up beside the house.

Since arriving she'd sunk into the embrace of the villa's familiarity, feeling that, after all, part of her old life remained. How precious that was.

For four days she'd let Dora feed her delicious food and done nothing more taxing than swim, sleep and eat.

Until today, when she'd woken to discover her brain teeming with ideas for her future. A future where, for a change, she did what *she* wanted, not what others expected.

A future here, at the villa that was her birthright.

For the first time since the funeral and her disastrous wedding day, Emma felt a flicker of her natural optimism.

Her training was in business and event management. She was good it and had recently won a coveted job at an upmarket vineyard and resort that she'd turned down when she married because she planned to move to Athens with Christo.

Emma suppressed a shiver and yanked her thoughts back to her new future.

She'd work for herself. The gracious old villa with its private grounds and guest accommodation was perfect, not only for holidays but as an exclusive, upmarket venue for private celebrations. That would be where she'd pitch her efforts.

Corfu was the destination of choice for many holiday makers. With hard work and good marketing, she could create a niche business that would offer a taste of old-world charm with modern luxury and panache.

It would be hard work, a real challenge, but she needed that, she realised.

Wasn't that what she'd always done? Kept herself busy whenever she faced another loss so that she had no choice but to keep going? It was her way of coping, of not sinking under the weight of grief. She'd adapted to a new life in a new state with her grandparents after her parents had died. She'd taken on the challenge of supporting Papou after her grandmother's death.

It was easier to focus on the ideas tumbling in her brain than the searing pain deep inside. To pretend Christo hadn't broken her heart and undermined her self-confidence with his casual dismissal.

Emma's mouth set in a tight line. She was still angry and hurt but now she had a plan, something tangible to work towards. That would be her lifeline. Today for the first time she no longer felt she'd shatter at the slightest touch.

Today she'd contact a lawyer about a divorce and getting back her property and—

'Miss Emma!'

She turned to see Dora hurrying around the rocks at the end of the private beach. Her face was flushed and her hands twisted.

Emma's heart slammed against her ribs. She knew distress when she saw it, had been on the receiving end of bad news enough to recognise it instantly. Foreboding swamped her. She started forward, hand outstretched, her beach towel falling to the ground. Was it her aunt or uncle? Not Maia, surely?

'I came to warn you,' Dora gasped. 'Your—'

'There's no need for that, Mrs Panayiotis.' The deep voice with its bite of ice came from behind the housekeeper. 'I'm perfectly capable of speaking for myself.'

Then he appeared—tall, broad-shouldered and steely-eyed. Christo Karides.

Emma's husband.

Her heart slammed to a stop, her feet taking root in the sand. The atmosphere darkened as if storm clouds had covered the sun. Was it the effect of his inimical stare? For a second she couldn't breathe, an invisible band constricting her lungs as she stared into that face, so familiar and yet so different.

Then, abruptly, her heart started pumping harder than before. She sucked in a faltering breath.

He was still the most handsome man she'd ever seen with his coal-black hair and olive-gold skin contrasting with clear, slate-blue eyes. Eyes that right now seared her right down to the soles of her feet.

Desperately Emma tried for dispassionate as she surveyed those proud features that looked like they'd been etched by a master's hand. Strong nose, square jaw, the tiniest hint of a cleft in that determined chin. Only the small silvered scar beside his mouth, barely visible, marred all that masculine perfection. Perversely, it accentuated how good-looking Christo really was.

Handsome is as handsome does. She could almost hear her grandmother's voice in her ears.

This man had proved himself anything but handsome. Or trustworthy. Or in any way worth her notice.

Wrangling her lungs into action again, Emma took a deep breath and conjured a reassuring smile for Dora. 'It's okay. Perhaps you'd like to organise some tea for us in the main salon? We'll be up shortly.'

As acts of hostility went, it was a tiny one, ordering tea when she knew Christo liked coffee, strong and sweet, but it was a start. Emma preferred conciliation to confrontation yet she had no intention of making him feel welcome.

Silence enveloped them as Dora hurried away. A silence Emma wasn't eager to break.

She told herself she was over the worst. The shock, the disillusionment, the shattered heart. But it was easier to believe it when the man she'd once loved with all her foolish, naïve hopes wasn't standing before her like an echo of her dreams.

Yet Emma wasn't the innocent she'd been a week ago. Christo Karides had seen to that. He'd stripped her illusions away, brutally but effectively. She was another woman now.

Pushing her shoulders back, Emma lifted her chin and looked straight into those glittering eyes. 'I can't say it's good to see you, but I suppose it's time we sorted this out.'

Christo stared at the woman before him, momentarily bereft of words for the first time in his adult life.

He told himself it was the shock of seeing her safe and healthy, after almost a week of worry. It had been uncharacteristic of gentle, considerate Emma to vanish like that, as all her friends and relatives kept telling him. He'd worried she'd been injured or even kidnapped.

Till she'd called her aunt and left a cryptic message saying she was okay but needed time alone.

Time alone!

His blood sizzled at her sheer effrontery.

What sort of behaviour was that for a bride? Especially for the bride of Christo Karides, one of the most sought-after bachelors in Europe, pursued wherever he went.

That had been another first—finding himself frantic with anxiety. Christo recalled the scouring, metallic taste of fear on his tongue and the icy grip of worry clutching his vitals. He never wanted to experience that again.

Nor did he appreciate being made a laughing stock.

Or enduring the questioning looks her relatives had given him, as if her vanishing act was *his* doing! As if he hadn't spent weeks carefully courting Katsoyiannis's delicate granddaughter. Treating her with all the respect due to his future wife.

Christo clamped his jaw, tension radiating across his shoulders and down into bunching fists.

It wasn't just discovering Emma hale and hearty that transfixed him. It was the change in her.

The woman he'd married had been demure and sweet-tempered. She'd deferred to her grandfather and been patently eager to please Christo, with her ardent if slightly clumsy responses to his kisses.

The woman before him was different. She sparked with unfamiliar energy. Her stance, legs apart and hands planted on hips, was defiant rather than placating.

The Emma Piper he knew was a slight figure, slender and appealing in a muted sort of way. This Emma even looked different. She wore a skimpy bikini of bright aqua. It clung to a figure far more sexy than he'd anticipated, though admittedly he'd never seen her anything but fully dressed. Her damp skin glowed like a gold-tinted pearl and those plump breasts rising and falling with her quick breaths looked as if they'd fill his palms to perfection.

A feral rush of heat jagged at his groin, an instant, unstoppable reaction that did *not* fit his mood or his expectations.

Christo dragged his gaze up to her face and saw her eyebrows arch in query, challenging him as if he had no right to stare.

As if she wasn't his runaway wife!

'You've got some explaining to do,' he murmured in the soft, lethal voice that stopped meandering board meetings in a second.

But, instead of backing down and losing the attitude, Emma jutted her rounded chin, lifted her cute, not quite retroussé nose in the air and planted her feet wider, drawing his attention to her shapely legs.

The heat in his groin flared hotter.

Slowly she shook her head, making her tangled, wet hair slide around her shoulders. Sunlight caught it, highlighting the dark honey with strands of gold he'd never seen before. But then they'd spent most of their time indoors, in her grandfather's house or at nearby restaurants. The bright Greek sunshine revealed details he simply hadn't noticed.

'You've got that the wrong way around.'

'Sorry?' Christo drew himself up to his full height, looking down on the slim woman before him. But, extraordinarily, she simply stared back, her mouth set in a mulish line. Her stare was bold rather than apologetic.

For a second he was so surprised he even wondered if the impossible had happened. If this wasn't Emma but some lookalike imposter.

But Christo Karides had never been one for fantasy. He'd been a pragmatist since childhood, with no time for fiction.

'Have you any idea how worried everyone was?' His

voice was gruff, hitting a gravelly note that betrayed the gut-deep worry he'd rather not remember. 'I even called the police! I thought you'd been abducted.'

He'd mobilised the best people to scour Melbourne and the surrounds, praying something terrible hadn't happened to his quiet little spouse.

There were ruthless people out there, including some ready to take advantage of a defenceless woman. His brain had kept circling back to the possibility that when he found her it would be too late. He'd never felt so helpless. The memory fed his fury.

'I rang my aunt to explain that I was safe.'

'You didn't ring *me*!' Christo heard his voice rise and drew a frustrated breath.

Was she wilfully misunderstanding? The woman he'd wooed had seemed reasonably intelligent and eminently sensible. Not the sort to disappear on her wedding day. He leaned into her space, determined to get through to her. 'I half-expected to find your abused body abandoned somewhere.'

He saw shock work its way through her, making her eyes round and her shoulders stiffen. Then she shook her head again as if dismissing his concern as nothing. 'Well, as you can see, I'm fine.'

'Not good enough, Emma. Not nearly good enough. You owe me.' An explanation to start with but far more after that.

'Oh, that's rich coming from you.' Her mouth curled up at one corner.

Was she *sneering* at him?

Christo covered the space between them in one long stride, bringing him close enough to inhale the scent of sea and feminine warmth that made something in his belly skitter into life.

Shackling her wrist with his, he tugged her close enough to feel the heat of her body.

'Stop it, Emma. You're my wife!'

Her voice when it came was so low he had to crane forward to hear it. Yet it throbbed with a passion he'd never heard from her. 'And how I wish I wasn't.'

Christo stared down at her. Never, in his whole life, had he met a woman who wasn't pleased to be with him. He'd lost count of the number who'd vied to catch his attention. Yet this one, the one he'd honoured with his name and his hand in marriage, regarded him as she would a venomous snake.

Had the world gone mad?

Where was his sweet Emma? The woman who revelled in his smiles, the gentle, generous woman he'd selected from all the contenders?

Her mouth twisted into a tight line as she stared down at his hand on her wrist. 'Let me go now. Marriage doesn't give you the right to assault me.'

'Assault? You have to be kidding.' His brow knotted in disbelief. As if he'd ever assault a woman!

'It is if I don't want to be touched and believe me, Christo, the last person on this earth I want touching me is you.'

Her voice was sharp with disdain and her nostrils flared as she met his stare. Something thumped deep in his chest at the unexpected, unbelievable insult.

Deliberately he dropped her hand and spread his empty fingers before her face. Anger throbbed through him. No, fury at being treated with such unprovoked contempt.

'Okay, no touching. Now explain.'

At last Emma seemed to realise the depth of his ire. The combative light faded from her eyes and her mouth compressed into a flat line. Abruptly she looked less fiery and more…hurt.

Christo resisted the ridiculous impulse to pull her close. He'd met enough manipulative women not to fall for a play on his sympathy.

'I know, Christo.' Her voice was flat, devoid of vigour. 'I know why you married me. There, is that enough explanation?'

'It's no explanation at all.' Yet the nape of his neck prickled.

It wasn't possible. He'd spoken of it to no one except Damen and then he'd ensured they were out of earshot. He'd left his blushing bride with her beaming family on the other side of the sprawling house.

He wasn't ashamed of what he'd done. On the contrary, his actions had been sensible, laudable and honourable. He'd offered marriage and the promise of his protection and loyalty to this woman. What more could she want? His actions had been spurred by the best of motives.

Except, looking into those wide, wounded eyes, Christo recalled her untutored ardour. Emma's shy delight at his wooing.

He'd told himself she didn't expect his *love*.

The old man had made it clear his granddaughter would marry to please him. Christo assumed she understood that behind the niceties of their courtship lay a world of practicality. That he'd wed for convenience.

But you never spelled it out to her, did you?

Christo silenced the carping voice.

No one who knew him would believe he'd been bowled over by little Emma Piper.

But Emma didn't know him. Not really.

For a second he wavered, surprised to feel guilt razor his gullet.

Till logic asserted itself. She'd chosen to marry him. He'd never spoken of love. Never promised more than he was willing to give.

Emma had flounced off in a huff and made him look like a fool. It was a part he'd never played before and never intended to play again.

Indignation easily eclipsed any hint of culpability. 'Nothing excuses what you did, Emma.'

'Don't try to put this on me, Christo. You don't even *want* me. You'd prefer someone beautiful and vivacious, like my cousin.'

Was that what this was about? He shook his head. He should have known this would boil down to feminine pique.

Emma was such an innocent that she didn't understand a man could be attracted to a woman and not act on that attraction. That a man of sense chose a woman who'd meet his needs.

Emma was that woman, with all the qualities he required of a mother for his ward. Even her defiance now just proved she had backbone, something he admired.

Plus she was more, he acknowledged. He met soft hazel eyes that now sparked with gold and green fire, feeling his blood heat as he took in her delectable figure and militant air. Christo acknowledged with a fillip of surprise that he wanted his wife more than he'd thought possible. Far more than he recalled from their restrained courtship.

There was a vibrancy about her, a challenge, a feminine mystique that called to him at the most primitive level. Gone was the delicate, compliant girl so perfect for his plans. This was a *woman*. Obstinate, angry and brimming with attitude. Sexier than he'd realised.

Lust exploded low in his body, a dark, tight hunger so powerful it actually equalled his fury.

'I married *you*, Emma. Not your cousin. I gave you my name and my promise.' How could she not understand what those things meant to him? 'That's far more important than any fleeting attraction.'

But Emma refused to be convinced. She shook her head,

wet hair slipping over her shoulders. Trails of sea water ran down from it to the miniscule triangles of her bikini top. Christo followed those wet tracks to the proud points of her nipples. Another wave of lust hit him and his flesh tightened across his bones as he fought the impulse to reach out and claim her.

'You're mine.' The words emerged as a roughened growl.

She stiffened, her chin jerking higher. 'Not for long. I'm filing for divorce.'

Like hell she would!

He'd carefully chosen Emma after considering all the options. Every reason he'd had for making her his wife still stood.

He needed her to make a real home instead of the bachelor flat he'd lived in for years. He needed her to be a mother to Anthea, providing a stable, caring environment for the little girl who was a stranger to him and with whom he had no hope of building a rapport.

Besides, Emma was *his*, and what Christo possessed he kept. It was in his nature.

Then there was today's revelation. That he wanted his wife with a hunger more powerful than he'd thought possible. That just standing here, fully dressed while she wore nothing but a bright bikini and a frown, brought him closer to the edge of his control than he'd been in years.

He intended to have her.

On his terms.

'File away, *wife*.'

He saw her flinch at the word and vowed that one day soon she'd purr at the sound of his voice. The thought of his runaway wife, eager for his touch, offering her delicious body for his pleasure, made the blood sing in his veins.

'But, before you do, I'd advise you to investigate the consequences. Divorce isn't an option.'

CHAPTER THREE

EMMA GROUND HER TEETH.

She was tired of men trying to rule her life. At least Papou had acted from love, not self-interest, wanting to see her 'safe' with a 'good' man before he died. Christo Karides had no such excuse. Her battered heart dipped on the thought but she refused to crumble as the familiar hurt intensified.

Instead she watched the tall figure of her husband turn and saunter back along the beach without a glance in her direction.

He should have looked out of place, ridiculously over-dressed, wearing a tailored dark business suit on a sandy beach. Instead, as she watched his easy stride, the latent strength in those broad shoulders and long legs, a thrill of appreciation coursed through her.

What a terrible thing desire was.

Her love, still fresh and new, had been battered away, swamped by pain and outrage. Yet standing in the sunlight, shivering not with cold but with a heat that she tried to label fury, Emma realised in horror that things weren't so simple.

She despised Christo Karides.

She loathed the cold-hearted way he'd set out to use her.

She vowed never to trust a word he said.

Yet as she watched him disappear around the end of the beach honesty forced her to admit she still desired him. That hadn't disappeared with her trust and her fool-ish dreams.

In Melbourne she'd thought the slow pace of his wooing sweet, proof he was considerate to her grief. At the same time she'd hungered for more than gentle caresses.

Now that hunger coalesced with the white-hot ire in her belly, producing an overwhelming mix of emotion and carnal need. She wanted to hurt him for the hurt he'd inflicted on her, yet at the same time she wanted…

Emma gritted her teeth and forced herself to breathe slowly.

She did *not* want Christo. She refused to allow herself to want him.

What she wanted, what she *needed*, was to free herself of him and this appalling marriage. She had plans, didn't she? An exciting scheme that would require all her energy and skill and which promised the reward of self-sufficiency in this place she loved.

Who did he think he was to decree divorce wasn't an option?

He might be the expert negotiator, the consummate sleazy liar who thought her easy pickings, but he was about to discover Emma Piper couldn't be steamrollered into compliance!

Forty-five minutes later Emma made her way from her bedroom to the salon with its expansive views of the sea.

Instead of hurrying to shower and dress, she'd taken her time, after having checked with Dora that Christo was, in fact, still on the premises. With that knowledge she'd locked her door and set about deciding what to wear.

Ideally she'd have worn a tailored suit, severe and businesslike. But Steph had persuaded her to splash out on new clothes for her honeymoon, reminding her that Papou would have wanted her to enjoy herself.

There was nothing businesslike in her wardrobe here. In the end, Emma gave up worrying about what impression her clothes might give Christo. She'd dress for herself.

The swish of her lightweight sea-green skirt around her bare legs reminded her of the holiday she was supposed to be enjoying. That she intended to enjoy as soon as *he'd* left. Her flat sandals were beach-comfortable rather than dressy and she wore a simple top that was an old favourite.

But she pulled her hair up into a tight knot at the back of her head and put on make-up, feeling that armour was necessary for the upcoming confrontation.

Ignoring the way the door knob slipped in her clammy palm, Emma opened the door and walked in.

To her surprise, Christo wasn't on his phone, absorbed in business, or pacing the vast room in obvious impatience.

Instead he stood at one end of the room, perusing the family photos her grandmother had collected. Generations of photos, mainly taken here on the Corfu estate to where Papou had brought his Australian bride before they'd decided to live full-time in her home country.

Christo swung around. His pinioning stare brought all the feelings she tried to suppress roaring into life.

After a moment Emma gathered herself. *She* had nothing to answer for.

She opened her mouth to ask if he needed another drink, then shut it again, annoyed that innate politeness made her even consider making the offer. Instead she crossed to a comfortable chair and sat.

'We need to talk.' Good. She sounded calm yet cool.

Silently one black eyebrow rose with arrogant query. The effect might have made her squirm if she hadn't been prepared.

'Or, if you prefer, I'm happy to finalise this via our lawyers.'

To Emma's chagrin that didn't dent his composure in the least. He strolled the length of the room, stopping to tower over her long enough to make her wonder if she'd made a mistake, taking a seat. Then, just before she shot to her feet, he settled into a chair, not opposite her but slightly to one side.

Emma silently cursed his game-playing and shuffled round to face him. Her skirt rode up at one side and she tugged it down, wishing she'd worn jeans instead.

Annoyingly, Christo looked utterly unruffled.

Until she saw the fire in his eyes and the determined set of his jaw.

Clearly he wasn't used to being crossed.

Good. It was time someone punctured his self-absorption.

'I'll file for divorce in Australia. I assume that's easiest.' Her tight chest eased a fraction as she spoke. It would be a relief to take action after days of doing nothing but grapple with disappointment and hurt. It was time to stop the self-pity.

'That's not a good idea, Emma.'

She frowned. 'I can't stay married to a man I despise.'

For an instant she thought she read something new flare in those heavy-lidded eyes. Something that sent a shiver tumbling down her backbone.

Emma sat straighter. What did she care if he wasn't used to hearing the truth about himself? He'd behaved appallingly and she refused to pretend otherwise.

'I know you're upset by your recent loss, so I'm willing to forgo the apology for your behaviour. But—'

'Apology for *my* behaviour?' She barely got the words out, she was so indignant.

Annoyingly, Christo simply nodded. 'Disappearing from your own wedding breakfast is hardly good form.'

She goggled at him.

'But your aunt and I convinced everyone you were completely overwrought. That the wedding had come too soon after the loss of your grandfather.' He spread his hands. 'I took the blame for wanting an early wedding, but your family understood and were very sympathetic.'

Emma opened her mouth then closed it again, feeling pressure build inside like steam in a kettle.

This was unbelievable!

'You made it sound like I had a breakdown? And they *believed* you?'

He shrugged, the movement emphasising the powerful outline of his shoulders and chest. 'What else could they believe? Your suitcase was gone, with your purse and passport.' His eyes narrowed to glowing slits that belied his relaxed pose. As if he were even now calculating how she'd managed to get away. Did he suspect Steph of helping? Had he bullied her into confessing? Steph hadn't mentioned it, but then she wouldn't.

'Once your aunt got that nonsensical message from you, of course she wondered.'

Emma shot to her feet. 'It wasn't nonsensical. I explained I needed time alone to think things through.'

Christo merely lifted those sleek black eyebrows and leaned back. 'Exactly. What sane woman would do that when she had a caring family and a brand-new husband to share her problems with?'

'Except *you* were the problem!' Emma heard her voice rise on a querulous note and swung away, pacing across to the window.

The view across the terrace to the private cove and bright sea did nothing to calm her fury. No one, not even her *papou* at his most obstinate, had got under Emma's skin the way this man had. Had she ever been so furious, her thoughts skittering so wildly?

How straightforward her world had been, how easy to be calm, before Christo Karides had slithered into her life.

Emma's heart hammered high in her chest at his gall, implying she was an emotional wreck who'd had a breakdown.

With a huge effort she pushed that aside. 'You said you'd worried I'd been abducted. But you knew I'd taken my luggage.'

Another nonchalant shrug. 'That wasn't clear at first. Your friend Steph didn't seem quite sure. And, even if you *had* left of your own free will, you could still have got into trouble. You're not used to being by yourself.'

Emma blinked. Christo made her sound like a child. Clearly he had no concept of the fact that she'd run Papou's house and some of his local investments for years. She'd chosen to live there for Papou's sake, not because she lacked independence.

Pride demanded she set the record straight.

She swung round and met that complacent, slate-blue stare, feeling the instant buzz of reaction as their gazes clashed. Immediately she changed her mind. Why explain to a man who'd soon be out of her life?

The notion eased the tightness cramping her chest and shoulders.

'We're wasting time. What's done is done.' It was time they moved on.

'I agree.' Yet the way Christo surveyed her, like a cat poised outside a mouse hole, warned her the next step wouldn't be so simple.

It was on the tip of her tongue to demand an apology but the way he sprawled there, ankles crossed nonchalantly, arms spread across the upholstery as he surveyed her, Emma knew she had no hope of getting satisfaction on that front.

The only satisfaction she'd get from this man was knowing she'd never have to see or hear from him again.

'It's in both our interests to end this quickly,' she began. 'Would an annulment be faster, do you know?'

'You think I'm an expert on unconsummated marriages?' For the first time Emma saw more than a flicker of annoyance in Christo's preternaturally still expression. Did he think she impugned his manhood by mentioning an annulment? She wouldn't be surprised. 'But I can tell you it would be a mistake.'

'How so?' Maybe annulments weren't simple after all.

'Because I refuse to consider it. Can you imagine the press furore if it became public?' He shook his head with grim disapproval.

'Frankly, I don't care. All I want is to be shot of you.'

His eyes narrowed to steely slits and his stare turned laser-sharp, scraping her throat and face. Emma crossed her arms and refused to look away.

'You've led a sheltered life. You have no idea how disruptive media attention can be till you've lived in the public eye.'

He was right. Emma had seen the articles about his business prowess, defying the odds when Greece's economy had faltered and his global investments had continued to return so spectacularly. And more, about his private life, all those assignations with beautiful women.

She shrugged one tense shoulder, her lips twisting in distaste. 'I'll cope, if it means ending this marriage quickly.'

'You really think you'd be able to deal with paparazzi camped at your door? Following you wherever you go? Digging up dirt—'

'There's no dirt to dig up!' At least not about her. Who knew what secrets Christo guarded?

'They'd invent something. The press are good at that.' He paused. 'Unless you have the power to keep them in check. As I have.'

Emma shuddered at the picture he painted of her hounded by photographers, of scurrilous stories in the tabloids, of friends and family pestered for interviews.

'If not an annulment, then a divorce.'

Christo spread his hands in mock sympathy. 'You'd still be hounded relentlessly.'

Emma lifted her chin. 'Maybe I'll sell my story to them

instead. Have you thought of that? I could make big bucks and then they'd leave me alone.'

For a second Emma thought he'd surge to his feet. She read the quickened pulse throbbing at his temple and the severe line of his mouth and knew Christo Karides wasn't used to such defiance.

Did people always do as he demanded? It was time someone broke the trend. Satisfaction filled Emma at the thought of being the one to disrupt his plans. She wasn't a pawn to be played to suit his schemes.

'Good try, Emma, but you won't do it.'

'You think you know me so well?' She sucked in a rough breath, trying to control the wobble in her voice. It didn't matter that fury, not hurt, made it unsteady. She hated the idea of seeming weak before this man. 'You have no idea who I really am. You never did.'

For what seemed an age, her surveyed her. 'I know you're a private person. You don't wear your heart on your sleeve.' He paused and she wondered, choking down hurt, whether he realised he was rubbing salt on her wounds.

For she *had* worn her heart on her sleeve. She'd been gullible, believing the unbelievable—that handsome, charming Christo Karides, with the world at his feet, actually cared for mousy little Emma Piper.

She spun on her heel and hurried across to the window, feigning interest in the view she knew as well as the back of her hand. It gave her time to deal with the honed blade of pain slicing through her.

Silence swallowed the room. When Christo spoke again his voice had lost that easy, almost amused cadence. 'What I mean is, you have more pride and integrity than to share anything so personal with the gutter press.'

Was he complimenting her? Emma blinked out at the sunlight glittering on the Ionian Sea and told herself it was too little and far, far too late.

'Coping with the press is a problem I'll deal with when I have to. My priority now is getting a divorce as quickly as possible.'

'That's not going to happen, Emma.'

Was that *pity* in his voice?

Her hackles rose. She swung round and was relieved to find she'd been wrong. That tight jaw spoke of impatience, nothing softer.

'You can prolong the process but you can't stop it.' That much she knew.

'You're my wife. We made vows—'

'Vows that meant nothing whatsoever to you!' Hearing her voice grow strident, she paused, hefting a shallow breath. Emma needed to stay calm, not fall apart. She'd run from him once, overwhelmed by the disillusionment that had rocked her to the core. She refused to give in to emotion now.

'I vowed to honour you, to cherish and look after you.' He'd never looked more proud or more determined. 'I have every intention of doing just that. This misunderstanding—'

'There's no misunderstanding. You cold-heartedly set about marrying me for a property deal.' As if she were a chunk of real estate! 'And to get a carer for your child.' Emma dragged in another breath but couldn't fill her lungs. 'Your baby is your responsibility. Yours and your lover's.'

An image filled her mind of Christo as she'd imagined him so often, sprawled naked in bed. But this time he wasn't smiling invitingly at her, he was kissing another woman. Their limbs were entwined and…

Emma banished the image and ignored the sour tang on her tongue that might, if she thought about it, be jealousy.

When she spoke again her voice was ragged. 'Together you need to look after the baby, not foist it on someone else.'

Her heart pumped an unfamiliar beat as adrenalin surged. Emma wasn't used to confrontation. She was a negotiator, a people pleaser, not a fighter. But something inside her had snapped the day she discovered Christo's motives and she still rode that wave of indignation.

She didn't know which was worse—that he'd played on her emotions and callously made her fall for him, or that he'd tried to palm his baby off on someone else. An innocent child deserved its parents' love.

What sort of world did the man inhabit? Surely one far removed from hers, where family and friends were everything.

Suddenly she realised he was on his feet, prowling towards her. Emma swallowed but stood her ground.

Fortunately he stopped a couple of paces away, so the illusion of distance held, though she caught a hint of the aftershave he used—cedar, spice and leather mingling with warm male skin. To her dismay, a little shimmy of appreciation shot through her.

'*Not* my child.' His voice was silky and soft but she heard the edge of anger. 'I would never be so careless.'

No, she realised, Christo was careful and calculating. Everything planned. Even down to choosing a suitable bride without a trace of sentiment or true feeling.

'And not a baby but a little three-year-old girl. The child is my stepsister's. She died recently.'

'I'm sorry.' Emma felt herself soften. She knew about loss, knew the struggle to keep going when everything seemed bleak.

Was it possible grief had made Christo act out of character? Could that explain…?

No. One look into those severely set features disabused her of that notion. She'd been right the first time. Christo didn't act in passion. He was a schemer who plotted every move.

'I barely knew her. Only met her once, years ago.'

'Yet you're now responsible for her child?' It made no sense.

He shrugged. 'There's no one else.'

It was on the tip of Emma's tongue to say that must be the case because no sane person would entrust an innocent child to such a man. But she bit the words back. She processed his words—*no one else*. But that was right: he was an only child and his parents were dead.

'The father?'

'If she knew who he was, she never said.' He paused. 'No one is going to come along and claim the girl.'

The girl.

He didn't even call the poor kid by her name.

Sympathy flashed through Emma. She understood what it meant to lose your family young. One day her parents had been there, seeing her off to school. The next, they'd been gone.

But she had her own battle to fight. She couldn't be swayed by emotion. That had been her downfall before.

'You both have my sympathy. But that's no reason to prolong this marriage.'

'Can you think of a better reason than to nurture a motherless child?'

How dared he talk of nurturing when his plan was to palm the child off on her?

'Of course I can. What about—?'

'Yes?' He leaned closer.

'Love', she'd been about to say. Marrying for true love.

But it hadn't been true and it hadn't been love, at least on his side. It had been a marriage of convenience.

As for her own feelings, Emma was ashamed of them. Especially since, despite everything he'd done, she wasn't as immune to this man as she wanted to be. Just as well there was no chance of him turning around and trying to persuade her he loved her. Even now she dreaded to think how effective he might be, given how he'd conned her the first time.

'I'm not getting into an academic discussion about marriage. I'm sorry for your niece...' *in more ways than one* '...but she's your responsibility. Take care of her yourself.'

Again, Emma felt that pang of sympathy for the little girl with no one but Christo to care for her. But he had money with which to bring in the best nannies. Once they were divorced, he'd find another wife. He'd proved how easy that was.

'Either agree to a divorce or leave. I have business to attend to.'

'Business?' His eyebrows shot up and for the first time she felt she'd truly surprised him.

'I have arrangements to make. A future to plan. A future without you.'

Stormy eyes surveyed her and she felt the force of his disapproval. No, more than disapproval. Sheer fury, if she read the thickening atmosphere correctly.

Once she would have hurried to placate, or at least redirect, that anger. Years living with Papou had made her adept at averting storms, finding ways of making him change his mind over time.

Today Emma stood her ground and rode the wave of displeasure crashing around her. If anything it buoyed her higher, knowing Christo could fume to no avail.

'These arrangements, do they require capital?' he asked finally.

'That's none of your concern.' He was stringing this out, hoping to undermine her confidence. Clearly he'd swallowed Papou's line about her needing to be looked after and guided.

As if part of her degree hadn't been in business management! Clearly Christo had missed that part of their conversation, probably distracted by planning how to tie her to his niece's nursery.

'On the contrary, it is my concern, if you're hoping to use your grandfather's property as capital.'

Something dropped hard through Emma's middle, like a stone plunging into a pool of arctic water. Chill splinters pricked her body.

She didn't like the triumph in Christo's eyes. As if he knew something she didn't.

But that was impossible. She already knew control of the valuable real estate in Athens had been handed to Christo on her behalf. Emma intended to change that, along with her married status.

'It's not my grandfather's property now. It's mine.' Her gaze swept the gracious room. This place, so full of precious memories, was her solace now, her home.

And more. It was her future. Her one asset, given her savings after years studying and looking after Papou were negligible. She'd get a loan using the property as collateral and invest it in the business she'd establish.

'If only that were true.' A deep voice cut through her thoughts.

She swung her head round to face him.

Either Christo had the best poker face in the world or he really did have bad news for her. Emma had a horrible feeling he was about to pull the rug out from under her feet...again.

She hiked her chin up, ignoring her stomach's uneasy roiling. 'If you have something to say, say it. I've had enough games.'

That sharp gaze held hers an instant longer then he shrugged. 'It seems your grandfather didn't tell you everything.'

That did it. Emma's stomach was now in freefall. She shifted her feet wider, bracing herself for the axe she sensed was about to drop, curling her hands into each other behind her back where Christo couldn't see.

'Go on.'

'He believed you needed a guiding hand. Which is why he left me in charge of the Athens property.'

'And?' Was he dragging this out to torment her?

'And your other inheritance, the estate here, is yours with the proviso that for the next five years any decision to sell or develop it, or take a loan against it, is subject to my approval. I have the right to veto any change of use if I don't believe it's in your long-term best interests.'

He smiled, a baring of white teeth that looked carnivorous rather than reassuring. 'Look on me as your business partner.'

Emma had been prepared for something but not this.

The blow struck at her knees, making them shake and threaten to collapse. Frantically she redistributed her weight, standing taller and hauling her shoulders back to glare at the man surveying her with that smug hint of a smile on his too-handsome face.

'I'll fight it. I'll challenge it in court.'

'Of course you will.' If she didn't know better, she'd almost have believed that soothing tone. 'But do you know how long that will take, or how much it will cost? How it will eat into your inheritance?' He paused, letting her digest that. 'You could lose everything.'

Main force alone kept Emma where she was. If she thought she had a hope of doing it, she'd have slammed a fist straight into Christo's smirking mouth.

She was still reeling, her brain whirring fruitlessly because, outrageous as it sounded, it was just the sort of thing her old-fashioned Papou might have done. Especially as he'd known his grandson-in-law-to-be was a commercial *wunderkind*.

He'd wanted to protect Emma. Instead he'd tied her to a man who wasn't fit to enter this house.

Belatedly she realised she should have insisted on reading every line of every legal document herself. More fool her!

'I'll still fight it.' Her voice was strained, her vocal cords pulled too tight.

'That's your prerogative.' Christo paused, that searing gaze stripping her bare. 'But there's an alternative.'

'What is it?' She didn't dare hope but she had to know.

'Simple. Meet my terms and you can do as you like with this place.' His mouth lifted at one corner in a hint of a smile but Emma knew in her very bones this would be anything but simple. 'I'll sign your inheritance into your control. All you have to do is fulfil your vows and live as my wife for a year.'

CHAPTER FOUR

'LIVE AS YOUR WIFE? You've got to be kidding.'

A flush climbed Emma's pale cheeks and her greenish brown eyes glittered more brightly than he'd ever seen.

She was a pretty woman but indignation made her arresting.

Christo surveyed her curiously. She vibrated with energy, her breasts heaving and her mouth working. She looked…full of passion. That hadn't been on his checklist.

The news he'd become responsible for his stepsister's child had come just before his visit to Australia. He'd picked Emma as a suitable bride because she'd make a good mother and a compliant wife.

But Emma was far more than either of those things, he realised. Instinct had drawn him to her with good reason. Her allure was more subtle and intriguing than surface glamour. His body tightened in anticipation.

He wanted his wife.

Wanted her more by the minute.

And he intended to have her. To salvage his pride after being dumped like an unwanted parcel at his own wedding. Because he had a score to settle. But above all because he'd desired her ever since their first gentle kiss. Her breathless ardour had unlocked something deep inside that had grown and morphed into something very like need.

'There are two things I never joke about. Business and family.' The first because it was his lifeblood, the second because he never made light of anything with such power to destroy.

'I *know* why you married me, remember? I *heard* what

you told your best man.' Emma's lips thinned as she pulled her mouth tight and the colour faded from her cheeks.

Christo didn't like her pallor. That drawn look made her seem fragile. Vulnerable. Reminding him that she looked that way because of him. He was responsible.

'I never lied to you.'

'Not specifically, but you made me believe—' She bit her tongue and looked away.

Christo could finish her sentence. He'd made her think he was falling for her. That he was a man capable of love.

Something dark slithered through his belly, drawing nausea in its wake. Without a second thought Christo stifled it. He didn't have the time or inclination for feelings. Nor for pointless self-recrimination.

'It's done now. And my offer is on the table.' An offer she *would* accept.

Her face swung round and the impact of all that barely contained emotion slammed into him. To his surprise, Christo welcomed it.

Because he'd rather have his wife angry than sad and defeated. It was a new concept. He filed it away for later consideration. Along with the dark shadow edging his conscience.

'You can't want me to live with you. I despise you.'

If Emma expected that to derail his plans, she really was an innocent. But then she hadn't come from his world but from what appeared to be a close, loving family. For a second Christo pondered what that would be like.

'You might be surprised at what I want and what I can live with. Besides, you owe me.'

'*I* owe *you*?' There it was again, that shimmer of defiance, that surge of energy that made his wife the most interesting woman he'd met in years. Even the fact that her vibrancy was due to inconvenient *feelings* didn't deter him.

'You gave your word. You made promises to me, Emma.'
He even enjoyed the taste of her name on his tongue.

How would that pale golden skin of hers taste?

'You really expect me to share a house with you?'

'And a bed.'

She goggled up at him as if he spoke Swahili instead
of English.

'You're not serious.' For the first time since he'd arrived
he saw her falter, grabbing the back of a nearby chair.

That hint of vulnerability ignited a trail of gunpowder
right through his considerable self-control. Was the idea of
sex with him really so appalling? He refused to believe it.

Christo enjoyed women, within strict parameters, and
he knew sexual attraction when he saw it. A week ago his
demure bride had been counting the hours till they were
naked together. Soon she would be again.

'But I am. You're mine, Emma, and I intend to have you.
At the very least you owe me a wedding night.'

Emma gripped the carved back of the antique chair and
willed the room to stop spinning.

This was crazy. Impossible.

Yet Christo Karides stood there looking as implacable
as ever. More so. Before the wedding she'd seen a gen-
tler, more restrained man. Now she saw the real Christo,
haughty and demanding. Over the top with his outlandish demands.

'You'd force me into sex?'

For the first time since he'd stalked along the beach—
sexy, brooding and starkly dangerous—she saw him recoil.

'I'd never force a woman. What sort of man do you think
I am?' He even had the temerity to look outraged!

'I know exactly what sort of man you are and the question stands.' Stronger now, Emma let go of the chair back

and slid her hands to her hips, adopting a combative attitude to hide her nerves.

'The answer is no. Sex with an unwilling woman... Never.' He shook his head, grimacing with distaste, and Emma felt the knot of tension in her chest loosen.

Then his gaze zeroed in on hers and suddenly she was short of breath.

'But you want me, Emma.' His certainty was infuriating and devastating, because it tapped into a weakness that shouldn't exist any more. She despised herself for feeling a tiny tug of response to his words. 'And I'll make sure you enjoy every single minute of it.'

His searing look clogged the protest in her throat. Or maybe it was her body's reaction to the images his words evoked. Heat blasted her. She reminded herself she hated him.

'If nothing else, I expect to share the wedding night we missed.' Something shifted in his eyes, something that spoke of calculation and determination. Emma shivered and rubbed her hands up her arms.

'You're demanding a year living with you and one night of sex? That's totally bizarre.'

He spread his arms, palm up. 'I need a wife to help my niece settle in. I have no skills with children.' His mouth twisted and for a second Emma thought she read something else in those slate-dark blue eyes. But it was gone before she could identify it. 'Even I know she needs more than a nanny. She needs a kind, caring parent figure to help her through the worst of the change. Don't forget, she's been through the trauma of losing her mother. *You* know how important it is that she has someone there for her.'

Damn the man. He was right. Emma didn't want to get involved. Yet she couldn't prevent a pang of sympathy for the little girl who'd lost her mother. And who apparently only had Christo to rely on! Poor kid.

Emma's bruised heart squeezed on the girl's behalf. At least when she was orphaned she'd had her grandparents, aunt and uncle. They'd closed ranks around her, a tight circle of love and support.

But she couldn't afford to be swayed, no matter how sorry she was for the child.

'As for us enjoying each other sexually...' Christo's deep voice cut through her thoughts. 'Once we begin, I'm sure we'll both want far more than one night. I'm confident we're well-matched physically.' His voice lingered on the last word, drawing unwanted heat from Emma's midsection down to the aching hollow between her legs. The sensation was new and unnerving. 'But I demand at least one night. Those are my terms.'

Despite her intention not to show weakness, Emma shuffled back half a step. 'It's preposterous!'

Christo said nothing, merely folded his arms over his chest and lifted one eyebrow.

Emma cast a look around the dear, familiar room. It would break her heart all over again to leave the family villa. But better that than what Christo proposed.

'I'll see you in court.' Her voice was crisp and decisive, despite the jittery whirl of emotions. 'Even if I have to walk out of here with only the clothes on my back. I'll go back to Australia, to my family and friends, and begin legal action to divorce and get back what's mine.'

Even if justice took years. Even if her inheritance was depleted in the meantime. She'd work and support herself.

She couldn't contemplate the alternative.

'That would be unfortunate.' Christo's arms fell to his sides, fingers flexing, and Emma wondered if he was restraining the impulse to reach for her. She pushed her shoulders back, meeting him eye to eye, knowing she had no alternative than to face him head on.

'I understand your uncle's business is dangerously over-extended. Even with the recent inheritance from your grandfather. If one of the investors were to withdraw it would be disastrous. The repercussions would impact not only him but your aunt and cousins. They could lose everything.'

Words choked in Emma's throat as her larynx tightened. She stared, wide-eyed, absorbing the threat in those softly spoken words.

Papou had said Christo was clever and daring. That he had a nose for business and a ruthless edge. Would he really be so ruthless as to destroy her family out of pique because she'd turned him down?

Emma wanted to doubt it but she couldn't take the risk.

'Are you *threatening* my family?'

She couldn't read anything in those arrogant features but determination.

'Do I need to?' He shook his head. 'There'd be no threat to them if you simply abided by your vows. With you as my wife I'd feel obliged to support your uncle if his company was in danger of floundering.'

Emma sucked in a breath. It was true her uncle's construction company had been through rough times. Now she thought about it, there'd been talk of Christo investing in it. But her head had been so full of other things that she hadn't paid much attention.

Now she was paying attention, far too late!

The walls pressed in on her. Or maybe it was the net this man had cast around her drawing tight.

Had Christo really invested in her uncle's company to ensure she complied? Or was it an empty threat?

Emma stared into eyes the colour of a stormy sky and felt something inside shrink. He was implacable, as merciless as a winter storm that wrought destruction on everything in its path.

Whether Christo had put money into the business for

purely financial reasons or as shrewd emotional blackmail didn't matter. Emma couldn't let him destroy her family.

'My grandfather was right about you. You really are utterly ruthless.' She grimaced, remembering Papou's enthusiasm for this man. 'To think he actually *respected* that. I'm glad he never had to find out what sort of man you truly are. You're a bully, Christo Karides.'

He didn't even blink, just stared back, eyebrows slightly raised, as if waiting for her to capitulate.

Emma swallowed hard, tasting a coppery tang. She realised she'd bitten down on her lip so hard she'd drawn blood and hadn't even felt the pain.

Frantically she ransacked her brain for an out. Something that would free her from this nightmare. But her luck had run out the day she'd fallen for this wolf in a tailored suit.

Why, oh, why had she broken the habit of a lifetime and acted rashly, marrying so quickly?

Because you fell for him. Hook, line and sinker.

The knowledge was acid, eating at her insides.

'I want to live here, in Corfu. Not in Athens.' Emma refused to let herself stop and think about the implications of what she was agreeing to.

'That works. My Athens apartment isn't designed for a child. This is much more suitable.'

If she needed anything to remind her of Christo's priorities, this was it. His first thought, his only thought, was for the child he expected her to mother. Everything else, even the sex he said he wanted, was secondary. But then he'd never really been attracted to Emma. The demand to share a bed was just male pique, because she'd escaped becoming another conquest.

She crossed her arms, clamping her fingers hard into bare flesh.

'Don't tell me you're willing to leave Athens?' Was

there, perhaps, hope that the threats had been a ploy? That
he had no intention actually of living with her?

'It's only an hour by plane. I'll spend week nights on the
mainland and the weekends here. That way Anthea will
have a chance to get used to me.'

For the first time he'd called his niece by her name.

And for the first time that Emma could recall, Christo
looked uneasy. His voice lacked its usual confident tone.

At the thought of spending time with Anthea? It didn't
seem possible. Christo was the most assured man she knew.

Emma didn't understand this cold-hearted stranger. He
showed no compunction or remorse about threatening her
in the most outrageous way, yet one little girl unsettled him?

But Emma had enough to deal with. Firmly she pushed
aside curiosity about the girl and her relationship with
Christo.

'I need time to consider.'

He shot his cuff and sliced a glance at his designer
watch. 'You have ten minutes.'

'Ten—'

'I have business to attend to. I need this wrapped up.'

As if she were an item on a meeting agenda, to be
crossed off before he moved onto the next matter.

Once, Emma would have murmured something plac-
atory and avoided further direct confrontation. But that
had been with her darling Papou, whose quick flares of
impatience had masked genuine worry for her future and
fear that his failing heart would give out before he saw
her settled.

Settled! With this arrogant...

'Of course making money is far more important than
dealing with real people.'

Her words brought that laser-sharp gaze back to hers.
Emma swallowed hard at the impact of that silent scrutiny.

Did he see past her bravado to the woman grappling with hurt and shock?

'Talk to your uncle, Emma. He and your aunt are real people, aren't they? Ask him how strong his business is.'

In the past Christo's deep voice had sent a thread of molten heat trailing through her insides. This time it created crackling frost along her bones.

Of course she'd talk to her uncle, but she knew he'd confirm what Christo said—that his company was vulnerable. One thing she'd learned, when Christo Karides wanted something, he didn't leave anything to chance.

'If I agreed to stay with you for a year...' Emma forced down bile '...how do I know I can trust you to keep your word?'

His eyebrows shot high, as if no one had ever questioned his integrity. She found that hard to believe.

'I'll have a contract drawn up.'

A contract setting out such a...personal deal? Her mind boggled. Yet she couldn't trust his word. Look at how he'd fooled her with his suave, persuasive ways.

'I won't sleep with you.'

He merely smiled. The man was so full of himself.

'It's not sleep I have in mind.' This time, despite every shred of indignation, despite his insufferable arrogance, Emma felt a tell-tale flutter in her belly. As if the woman who'd loved and longed for this man was still here, eroding the foundations of her anger.

'The contract will arrive tomorrow.' He looked as if he was going to say more then shook his head. 'Anthea and I will be here on the weekend.' Then, before Emma could find any words, he strode from the room.

Sure enough the next afternoon a courier arrived.

Emma was dishevelled after hours trying to quell her fury and fear by exploring the estate from top to bottom.

She'd checked out every inch of the villa, its outbuildings and the neglected villa next door which Papou had bought and hadn't got around to renovating. If Emma was to turn this into an exclusive small function centre, that second villa would be a wonderful asset.

If she was still here in Corfu.

If she didn't cut her losses and go home.

Except she'd called her uncle and knew she had no choice. He'd confirmed that Christo had invested heavily in the family construction company. He'd even added that things would be tight without Christo's support.

Support!

Emma shivered and looked down at the sealed envelope in her hands. It felt like a ticking time bomb. Her hands were clammy and, despite the cool breeze through the open front door, she was overheated.

The sound of the courier's car accelerating onto the main road broke her stasis. She tore open the envelope.

There it was, in excruciating detail. Christo had signed over control of the Corfu property, and a sizeable share of the expected profits of the Athens redevelopment. In return she'd live as his wife for a year. She'd take no lovers. She'd appear with him as necessary in public and behave with expected decorum. She'd accommodate his niece. She'd grant no media interviews about their relationship, ever.

And she'd have marital relations with Christo Karides at least once.

He'd actually had the gall to include that in the contract! His signature slashed the page just below it.

All Emma had to do was sign and she'd have the property that should already be hers.

For long moments she stared at the document. Then something snapped. Emma shoved the contract back into the envelope, breathing hard.

Dared she?

But what alternative did she have?

She'd keep this safe as proof of her husband's intentions and manipulations in case she needed it in a future court case. She'd delay filing for divorce till the twelve months was up. She'd give his niece a home, poor little kid. She'd even put up with Christo staying every weekend.

But as for the rest... She might be cornered but she had her self-respect. Emma refused to sign. She and Christo Karides would be married in name only.

If that wasn't good enough, she'd swallow her pride and go to the press. It was a distasteful last resort. Emma valued her privacy and shuddered at the thought of laying herself bare for the world to read about. But selling her story might provide enough money to tide her family and her over till she won back what was hers.

For the first time since Christo had sauntered back into her life, all arrogance and outrageous demands, hope stirred.

She could do this. She *would* do it.

She'd throw herself into creating her business and at the end of the year she'd get her property back. Christo was bluffing about them having sex. He had to be. It was just bruised masculine pride talking.

He'd only drawn up the contract to satisfy her concerns that he'd renege on the deal. Now she had his signature proving he intended to hand over the property, she was safe. She had to believe that.

All she had to do was endure fifty-two weekends without trying to kill her infuriating, selfish, diabolically annoying husband.

CHAPTER FIVE

THE FOLLOWING SATURDAY morning Emma and Dora stood in the villa's entry, watching a driver open the back door of a long, black limousine.

Emma's breath snagged in the back of her throat and her pulse pounded, waiting for Christo to emerge. But it wasn't he who appeared. Or a little girl.

It was a woman, and what a woman.

Emma had told herself nothing Christo did now could surprise or hurt her.

She'd been wrong.

Watching long, toned legs appear, narrow feet in high-heeled sandals and a tall, sinuous figure in a tightly fitted dress, everything inside Emma stilled. Then the woman turned to look about her and the sun danced on glossy sable waves that cascaded around slim shoulders and framed a face so beautiful it belonged on a magazine cover.

Emma felt as though she'd been slapped in the face.

He'd brought his lover with him. To her home.

Her home!

Abruptly the nerves making her anxious melted away, replaced by incandescent fury.

Emma's gaze locked on the woman, so she didn't even notice Christo emerge from the car, or the little girl who stood awkwardly between the two adults, until Dora started forward with words of welcome.

Emma blinked and looked again, taking in the tableau before her in freeze frames.

The beauty was looking tentatively at Christo, who frowned mightily. But he ignored the woman, his attention fixed on the child who must be Anthea. A little girl with tight brown plaits and pale, skinny hands clasped before her. She didn't look at either of the adults beside her, but stared warily at Dora, who smiled and welcomed them.

Finally Christo turned, his eyes locking on Emma's. Even braced for it, she was stunned by that sudden sizzle of connection. No, not connection, she told herself. Fury.

She stalked forward, intending to confront him, only to falter when Anthea shrank back, not towards Christo or his girlfriend, but towards the solidly built driver.

Emma's anger ebbed as other emotions rose. Guilt for scaring the kid with her sudden surge of movement. Sympathy and remembered heartbreak. Memories of grief and insecurity. Of feeling alone in a world that didn't make sense after her parents had died.

Emma dropped to a crouch before the little girl, discovering soft brown eyes, a smattering of freckles and a mouth that hooked up at one side as she bit her cheek.

'Hello,' she said quietly. 'I'm Emma. You must be Anthea. Is that right?'

Silently the girl nodded, her eyes wary and huge. Emma's chest tightened as if her ribcage shrank around her heart. She watched Anthea's hands tighten convulsively on each other and repressed a frown. At the very least the poor kid should have a teddy or something to cuddle given none of the adults with her could be bothered offering comfort.

'Do you like rabbits?' Emma asked impulsively, thinking of the toy rabbit she'd rediscovered in the room she'd used as a girl. Washable and soft, it had survived years of snuggling almost intact.

Anthea didn't answer, just lifted her shoulders in a tiny shrug and bit her lip harder. Emma waited for one of her companions to step in and reassure her. But a quick glance showed Christo standing back as if the girl had come with a health warning. The woman was no better, busy surveying Christo through her lashes.

'Would you like to come inside and see one?' Emma smiled. 'He can't hop or eat grass but he likes spending time with little girls and he loves being cuddled.' She paused. 'Do you like giving cuddles?'

'I don't know.'

The whisper stilled the last buzz of Emma's dying temper. She forgot about her unwanted adult guests and focused totally on the too-serious face of the girl before her. The girl she hadn't wanted to build a close relationship with, because she knew it could only lead to pain when they went their separate ways after twelve months. Emma had told herself it was up to Christo to forge a bond with his niece, not her.

Now that notion died an abrupt death. Emma couldn't ignore this little girl whose reserve and tension told its own sorry tale. She wanted to wrap her close and tell her everything was going to be okay. Instead she kept her tone light.

'Then let's find out, shall we? I'll take you to him if you like.' She rose and reached out her hand.

Anthea stared at it as if she'd never held an adult's hand in her life. She shot a swift, upward glance at the others, almost as if expecting reproach, then reached out and touched Emma's fingers.

Anthea's tiny hand was cool in hers but Emma was careful not to betray surprise at that or the tremor she felt pass through the little girl. Instead she smiled and turned towards the door, catching Dora's eye. The housekeeper would see to the adults. Right now the priority was this little waif and making her feel comfortable.

The enormity of the situation hit Emma again, making her falter for a second. She was about to take on responsibility for a child, a child who, obviously, needed love and lots of it.

But Emma couldn't turn her back on the girl. This had nothing to do with Christo's threats. It was about recognising the blank shock on Anthea's face, the feeling of loss and fear, the dreadful uncertainty.

Emma had been there. She couldn't treat the girl as a pawn in some power play.

She stepped into the house, Anthea tentatively returning her grasp. 'He's a very special rabbit, you know. He's lived here for a long time. I hope you like him.'

Christo surveyed the spacious bedroom suite he'd been given and tried to turn his mind to practicalities, like Wi-Fi access. Instead he found himself staring at the perfect curve of blue-green sea in the cove, his thoughts in turmoil.

Not only his thoughts. His gut roiled with unfamiliar emotion.

It wasn't the Ionian Sea he saw. It was Emma crouching before his niece, cajoling her into a response after hours of the kid being silent and withdrawn.

He'd known all along that Emma would make a great carer. She was warm-hearted and generous. Her body language around the girl had been fiercely protective, yet her expression had been soft, something that he was sure would turn into love one day.

His gut clenched.

Christo couldn't remember ever being so close to such naked maternal tenderness. Any sort of tenderness, come to that. Except the fleeting sense of intimacy he got from sex. The short afterglow that made the mirage of emotional intimacy seem almost as tangible as physical closeness. Until logic kicked in, reminding him it was a fantasy.

Impatient, Christo marshalled his thoughts, ignoring the unfamiliar pang as he recalled Emma's expression and his unwarranted reaction.

He opened the French doors and stepped onto the wide terrace.

Emma's reaction might have been all he could wish for but Anthea's nanny was another matter.

He gritted his teeth at the thought of the woman who'd been recruited so carefully to provide the best care for his step-niece. He'd left the recruitment to experts. After all, what did he know about selecting a child minder?

Now he saw he should have taken a hand, vetting the applicants himself. The woman with such excellent experience and references—the woman who had been soberly dressed and devoted to her charge, the time they'd met previously—had transformed utterly. He'd been confronted at the airport by a siren more interested in batting her eyelashes at him than caring for Anthea.

He sighed and shrugged out of his jacket, dropping it over the back of a chair. He'd sometimes had the same problem with temporary office staff. Women who were all business till the day they found themselves alone with the boss. A boss who regularly featured on those 'hottest, richest bachelor' lists.

The question was, did he fire her effective immediately or give her notice? It would take time to replace her. And even he, used to others doing his bidding, didn't expect his wife to take sole charge of Anthea.

Anthea. Who looked so like her mother.

Christo shoved his hands in his pockets and stepped out onto the grass. He'd deal with the nanny later. With everything later. For now he needed fresh air.

Ever since he'd boarded the plane and seen Anthea with her big brown eyes, Christo had felt claustrophobic to the point of nausea.

It was pathetic. It was all in his head. Yet he felt the tension notch higher with each breath.

Being with the child brought back memories he hadn't revisited in years.

Turning his back on the house, he lengthened his stride.

* * *

'Where have you been?'

Christo stopped in the shade of a wide, twisted olive tree, locating the source of the question.

Emma. His wife.

Heat ignited low in his abdomen. Satisfaction. And more besides.

Instead of being pinned up, her hair was around her shoulders in a drift the colour of wild honey. Was it the sunshine that made it glow? In wintry Melbourne the colour had been more subdued. Like the woman.

Maybe the difference was her bright, summery clothes. In a sleeveless wrap-around dress the colour of apricots, she looked good enough to eat. Especially as the light fabric skimmed breasts and hips and that narrow waist which had so fascinated him when he'd held her close.

Christo's groin grew heavy. She stood with arms folded and hip jutting in a confrontational stance that triggered a reaction deep in his psyche. Something he could only describe as very primitive and utterly masculine.

'Walking,' he murmured, watching her eyes flare brighter. As if she struggled to contain her emotions.

Was that what she'd done before? Kept her emotions under wraps?

The woman he'd courted in Australia had been reserved and eager to please. Christo had thought he wanted the quiet, compliant Emma. But there was a lot to be said for vivacity. For passion.

'You don't think it would have been helpful if you'd stayed with Anthea? Helped her settle in?'

Christo settled his shoulders back against the rough bark of the tree and slowly crossed his arms. 'You were doing a fine job. Better than I could have done. My skills don't lie in that direction.' Give him business any day. Wrangling a profit in a difficult commercial environment was far easier than dealing with family or feelings.

Emma shook her head gain, dark blonde waves slipping around her shoulders. 'That's no excuse. You should have been there. You're her uncle.'

Step-uncle. But Christo didn't correct her.

'It's not me she needs. It's someone like you, with a knack for dealing with children.'

'Don't think you can get out of your responsibilities so easily.' Her voice was low and even but determined. 'You need to build a relationship with her. When we divorce, I won't be around to take care of her.'

There'd be no divorce.

Christo planned to keep Emma as his wife. Once she got used to the idea, once he'd taken her to bed, she'd change her mind. It might be his money and looks that initially attracted women, but he knew how to satisfy them.

Pleasure stirred at the memory of Emma on their wedding day. Her breathless anticipation. The flurry of nerves that barely concealed her desire for him.

All he needed was patience, time to remind her how much she wanted him.

There'd be pleasure too in having what she'd denied him when she'd run off, leaving him to explain the inexplicable to her friends and family. Runaway bride, indeed! Did she really think she could make a fool of him and not pay? Did she think he had no pride?

'I have every intention of developing a relationship with her.' Though the thought of it made him feel...

No. Better not to examine that too closely. He knew his duty and he'd do it.

'Well, you haven't got off to a good start.'

Christo shrugged. 'Some things take time.' Such as seducing a woman who needed the reassurance of a gentle touch. He read more than anger in Emma's obstinate stance and quickened breathing. There was awareness. How could he not notice when it crackled in the air between them?

'They'd go far better without your girlfriend here.' The words emerged through clenched teeth. Emma bit the words out.

Jealousy?

Despite the tension he'd fought these last hours, Christo felt delight unfurl.

'She's not my girlfriend.'

'She sure fooled me.'

Emma's chin swung higher. It wasn't Christo's companion who'd made a fool of her. It was her own husband. How she hated that word. Husband. Almost as much as she hated the fact she'd been stupid enough to marry him. She must have been out of her mind!

Now he'd brought his lover here. She'd heard about open marriages but this was the man who just days ago had demanded sex as his marital right!

As if all that weren't enough, there was yet another sting in the tail.

Despite the different colouring, one brunette and one redheaded, there was a strong similarity between the woman who'd stepped out of the limo and Emma's cousin, Maia. The gorgeous cousin with whom Christo had admitted he'd like to have an affair.

Both women were tall, sexy in a sultry, almost earthy way, yet with a sophistication Emma couldn't hope to match.

Plain Emma. Ordinary Emma. Emma the 'nice' girl. Emma who played by the rules and didn't like to upset people who cared for her.

She dug her fingers into her upper arms, fighting a wave of reckless anger. Losing her temper wouldn't help.

Yet, now she'd met Christo's 'type' and realised how far she was from the sort of woman he wanted, it was a battle to retain some surface calm. Because it brought home how ridiculous her dreams of happy-ever-after had been.

'Emma?' He straightened from the tree and moved closer, forging a path through scarlet poppies and smaller wildflowers. In the dappled light of the olive grove she almost believed that was regret on Christo's face. Except she'd had enough of self-delusion.

'That's far enough.'

He halted before her, his gaze clear and open, as if he'd never deceived her.

'She's Anthea's nanny, not my lover.'

Emma snorted. 'Even I'm not that gullible.'

'But I was. Or at least, the recruitment expert was.'

Something about his tone of voice, the jarring note that sounded like discomfort, as well as annoyance, stopped Emma's scornful reply.

This was the first time Christo Karides had admitted being anything other than in control. Was it a trick?

He curled his hand around the back of his neck. The action dragged his casual shirt up, stretching it across his wide chest.

Emma stared then raised her gaze to his face, telling herself it was the drowsy afternoon heat of the sheltered grove that made her feel warm.

'You're telling me she really is a nanny? She doesn't look or act like one.'

'The only other time I met them, she wore flat shoes, hair pulled back and her outfit was sensible, not—'

'Sexy?' Emma arched her eyebrows. 'Surely you noticed she couldn't take her eyes off you? She didn't even glance at Anthea.' Outrage on behalf of the bereaved little girl cut through Emma's hurt. They were both victims of this man.

'Oh, I noticed. *Today.*' His tone was grim. 'But she wasn't like that the other time. Then she was wonderful with

Anthea. Attentive and reassuring. She perfectly matched her excellent references.'

Emma frowned, finally registering what Christo had said a moment ago. *The only other time he'd met them.*

It wasn't just the nanny he'd met only once. It was his niece too. No wonder Christo and Anthea behaved like complete strangers. Yet did that explain his grim expression as he'd surveyed the little girl?

Slate-blue eyes caught and held hers. 'Today I saw a different side to her.' He lifted one shoulder in a half-shrug and Emma realised he was still talking about Anthea's nanny. 'It happens. Women deciding to make a play for a rich man who'll be a meal ticket. But I confess this time I was taken completely by surprise.'

Emma stared back at this man who took such things in his stride. A light breeze riffled his jet-black hair and the shifting shadows cast those high, carved cheekbones in stark relief, accentuating his hard male beauty.

She knew they came from different worlds but to accept such games as inevitable? 'If that's normal in your world, then I pity you.'

Something shifted in his face. His expression closed, turned still. For just a second Emma sensed she'd hit a nerve. Or had she imagined it?

'I'm not interested in sleeping with the hired help.' His voice was chill, sending a shiver tracking over her bare arms and neck. 'I never mix sex and business. Besides, I have a wife. Remember?' The way his voice dipped suddenly took Emma's stomach with it, diving low in a giddy swoop. 'What I want is someone I can trust to care for Anthea. She needs it, poor kid, after what she's been through.' He paused, as if side-tracked by his thoughts.

'You mean more than losing her mother?' Emma didn't know what prompted her words. A parent's loss would make any kid withdrawn and wary. Emma was certain her own early losses had affected her that way too. Yet after just a short time with Anthea she wondered at her level of self-containment, and the bruised expression in her eyes, as if expecting the worst at any moment.

Christo fixed her with a hard stare, as if daring her to go on. For answer she simply stared back.

Finally he sighed and shoved his hands deep in his trouser pockets. 'It's as well you know.' He paused and paced away, as if too restless to stand still. 'Anthea was living with her mother, my stepsister, in the USA.'

'Not in Greece?' But then that would explain why Anthea had responded easily when Emma had spoken to her in English.

'My stepmother and stepsister were American. It was decided Greece didn't suit my stepsister.' To Emma's astonishment, she saw Christo's mouth work, tugging down in a grimace before flattening into a grim line.

Her curiosity rose. She was about to ask what that meant when Christo continued. 'She went to live with relatives in the States.'

'Instead of staying with her mother and your father?' It seemed odd.

'Yes.' His tone put off further questions. 'She lived there till she died recently. Sadly, it wasn't a settled life. She was…troubled.' There it was again, that slight hesitation that made Emma more rather than less curious about his choice of words.

'Put plainly, she became addicted to drugs and alcohol. As far as I can tell, she never lived with Anthea's father, whoever he was.'

'You weren't in contact with her?'

Christo shook his head and turned to survey the villa through the trees. Was it her imagination or did he deliberately avoid her eyes?

'I only ever saw her once, years ago. I never heard from

her after she left.' He opened his mouth then closed it again. Had he been going to add something?

Emma pushed the idea aside. The issue now was Anthea, not Christo's relationship with her mother.

'Anthea lived with an addict?' Her heart sank as she imagined the sort of life the little girl had experienced.

Christo nodded, the movement abrupt. 'They moved a lot and I suspect she was neglected.'

Emma looked at that hard face, the profile made severe by tension, and realised that behind the adamantine stillness of his features Christo was distressed.

It made him suddenly, unexpectedly, human.

A flurry of warmth rushed through her. An unwanted stirring of sympathy.

She'd thought of him as a liar and a cheat. Seeing evidence of a softer side was unsettling.

'I should have followed up. I shouldn't have assumed she was okay.' The words were so quiet they melded with the sigh of the breeze through the silvered olive leaves.

Emma was puzzled. She'd assumed Christo and his stepsister had been young when they'd met. That Christo hadn't been responsible for her.

He turned back, those dark blue eyes searing in their intensity. 'Anthea hasn't had the advantage of a stable home or family. That's one of the reasons I want her settled with someone who can nurture her.'

Emma, in other words.

Indignation stirred anew. She wasn't some mail-order bride to be brought in to fill a gap. Yet her anger was muffled this time by the story she'd heard.

She understood Christo's desire to look after his niece. She even applauded it. Except for the ruthless way he'd lied to her, making her believe he wanted *her*.

'In that case, you need an excellent nanny. You can't rely on me long term.'

To her surprise, Christo inclined his head. 'Before you arrived I was debating whether to dismiss this nanny immediately. But that would leave you in the lurch when I go back to Athens.'

'You were concerned about me?' His consideration surprised her. Hadn't he acquired her for that very purpose?

Familiar hurt jabbed her. That was all she was to him, a convenient business acquisition, bringing him property and the mothering he wanted for Anthea. Even his demand for sex had been an afterthought, driven by annoyance that she'd defied him. She knew one thing for sure. She wasn't his type.

'Of course.' His gaze held hers. 'I never expected just to foist Anthea onto you. It would be unreasonable to expect you to care for her twenty-four hours a day. As my wife, you'll have other things to do with your time. And Dora is already busy enough.'

For a moment there Emma had actually started to warm to Christo. Until the reference to her being his wife. As if she had no other purpose in life.

'Actually, I'm going to be busy setting up my business. I won't have time for much else.'

Those penetrating eyes surveyed her for silent seconds and Emma wondered what he read in her face.

'All the more reason to find reliable help for Anthea.' Emma couldn't argue with that. 'The difficulty is that when I dismiss this nanny it will take time to find someone suitable.'

'You could look after her yourself.'

Black eyebrows winged up that broad forehead. 'I'm many things, Emma, but experienced in caring for traumatised children isn't one of them. Even if I trashed my schedule for the next several weeks to be with her, I wouldn't be suitable.'

'It's not a matter of being suitable. It's about providing warmth and love.'

Christo didn't answer. Didn't so much as blink.

He was right, Emma realised with icy clarity. Christo didn't do love. Little Anthea needed more than he could provide.

'Don't sack the woman. Give her another chance.' She surprised herself with the words.

'Are you serious?'

'You said yourself that she did a good job before. Maybe today was an aberration she's already regretting. We all make mistakes.'

Emma should know. This man had been the biggest mistake of her life. She knew how he could turn a woman's head.

'I could put her on notice. Spell out the boundaries to her,' he said slowly, as if thinking through Emma's suggestion. 'After all, she's the only one of us that Anthea has known for more than a couple of hours.'

'In that case, definitely give her a second chance. For Anthea's sake.'

He frowned. 'We'll have to keep a close eye on the situation. I won't allow Anthea to be neglected again.'

Did he notice that he'd said 'we'? It sounded as if he intended to take an active role in monitoring the situation. Perhaps he wasn't as cold-hearted as he seemed.

'If she doesn't live up to expectations, you can hire someone else. You could even tell your recruitment people that you may need a replacement if this one doesn't work out so they can check their books.'

'This time I'll vet the applicants personally.' Christo nodded. 'Thanks, Emma. It's a good, practical suggestion.'

Suddenly he smiled, a grin that transformed his features from sombre to breathtakingly attractive. It made Emma's pulse trip and stumble, then continue erratically.

'See how well we work together when we try? It just proves how perfectly matched we are.'

CHAPTER SIX

PERFECTLY MATCHED!

How dared Christo pretend they were any such thing?

Emma lay on her bed, fuming. No matter how she'd tried, she hadn't been able to sleep.

To her dismay she'd shared dinner alone with Christo. Anthea was too little to stay up and, after an interview with Christo, her nanny had elected to stay and watch over her. Dora had refused, point blank, to break a lifetime's habit and join them in the dining room.

Christo had been all easy charm, reminding her of their courtship in Australia. He'd complimented Emma on the villa and won Dora over with praise of her food and her home-made kumquat liqueur. It was hard to believe he was the same man who'd threatened blackmail to get Emma into his bed.

But she'd been taken in by him before. She refused to fall for that charade again. He might seem considerate but beneath lay a heart as cold as a steel trap.

Except where his niece was concerned. And, Emma suspected, his stepsister. There'd been something about his expression when he'd spoken of her…

Emma rolled her eyes, disgusted at her eagerness to find good in the man. She turned over and punched her pillow, trying to get comfortable.

It was impossible. Christo Karides kept invading her brain. It was bad enough when he'd been in another country, or on the mainland. Having him under the same roof made her edgy.

She told herself she felt indignant at him making himself at home, as if he were an invited guest instead of an unwanted husband.

There it was again. That shudder of repugnance at the word 'husband'.

But Emma was always brutally honest with herself, even if she'd spent years smoothing over prickly issues with her *papou*. That wasn't all she felt. There was a sliver of something else.

It had been satisfying this afternoon, discussing Anthea and her needs with him, hearing his thoughts and having him take her input seriously. That reminded her of their time in Melbourne, when he'd been not only solicitous but interested. She'd thought that had all been false. Now she wondered.

Emma bit her lip. She was going around in circles. She couldn't trust Christo Karides. The truly unnerving thing was that, despite everything, part of her wanted to.

On a surge of impatience, she flung back the covers and got up, grabbing the robe from the bottom of the bed.

Her mouth twisted as she put it on and cinched it around her waist. Steph had helped her choose it, and the matching nightgown of champagne silk and gossamer-fine lace for her trousseau. Emma had never owned anything like them in her life.

She'd imagined wearing this on her wedding night. Imagined Christo peeling it off as he kissed her in places she'd never been kissed before.

The thought raised gooseflesh on her skin, from her thighs to hips and abdomen.

Spinning on her heel, Emma marched across the room and wrenched open the door to the balcony. She needed to think about something other than Christo. She'd count stars. That would keep her busy for the next hour or two.

There wasn't much moon and as the village was around the headland there was no light pollution. Just the inky-dark sky, the sigh of the sea and thousands upon thousands of stars.

Emma crossed to the railing and breathed deep. Funny that she'd never realised how much she missed this place till she returned. The scent of the sea was so evocative, mingling with the perfume of blossom and something else she couldn't name. A spicy aroma that tugged a cord low in her belly. She closed her eyes and inhaled through her nose, her brow crinkling in concentration. It was tantalisingly familiar and deeply attractive. She just couldn't place it.

'Hello, Emma.' Christo's voice, warm as melted chocolate, enveloped her. 'Couldn't sleep?'

She spun, one hand grabbing the railing for support, the other automatically closing the neck of her robe.

He stood a little way along the balcony. The private balcony accessed only by the master suite and one extra room where Papou had occasionally slept when Grandma had been ill and easily disturbed.

Emma blinked, but he was still there. Christo Karides, looking as she'd never seen him before. The light was too dim to read his expression but there was still a lot to see. A lot of naked flesh. He wore only loose, low-slung trousers that rode his hips and looked on the verge of sliding down long, hard thighs.

She swallowed abruptly and yanked her gaze up. But there was his bare torso. The starlight picked out sculpted lines and curves that spoke of power and pure eroticism.

He looked wonderful fully clothed. But half-naked, he was stunning. She'd dreamed of him nude so often but it was a shock to discover how compelling the sight of that bare body was. How it smashed through her anger and drilled down to the burning truth within her. That physically, at least, she'd never stopped craving this man. Even the rounded angles, from shoulders to arms and the symmetry of that tall, muscular frame, were too much.

Emma's breath disintegrated in an audible sigh and she swung away to stare at the sea. But her precarious calm was gone. She heard nothing over her pulse's catapulting rhythm.

And the tiny voice in her brain that spoke of want.

'What are you doing here?' She turned her head in his general direction, but not far enough to see him. This blast of weakness was too appalling. She refused to feed it.

'Like you, I had trouble sleeping.' He paused but only for a fraction. 'Perhaps we should find something to do together that will tire us out.'

Emma ignored the amusement in his tone and the blatant innuendo. That didn't deserve an answer.

But she couldn't ignore the unnerving hollow ache low in her body. Or the spiralling heat. It was as if at twenty-two her body had suddenly lost all connection with her brain, or with that part of it devoted to rational thought. She despised this man. She never wanted to see him again. But her long-dormant libido hadn't got the message yet. Once roused by him, it was still alive and eager.

'I mean, what are you doing here, in this part of the house? We prepared a different suite for you.'

'And it was charming. But totally unsuitable.'

Emma was on the point of swinging round to look at him when she changed her mind. Instead she anchored her fingers on the decorative ironwork railing and clenched her teeth.

'Why?'

'Because I asked Dora where your room was and told her I wanted to be next door. I refuse to sleep in the wing furthest from my wife. As you said, we have a relationship to forge.'

'I was talking about you and Anthea.' Her fingers tightened till they felt numb.

'Us too, Emma.' His voice slid easily to that *faux* intimate note that in the past had drawn her in so easily. The note that she'd innocently thought signalled genuine caring. She knew better now.

'There's no need for that. It's a marriage in name only and it will last just twelve months.'

'You know that's not true. You know there's more between us.'

Unable to contain herself, she spun round to face him. He'd moved closer, so close she could almost touch him. She jerked her gaze up and caught the glitter in his eyes.

'There won't be anything more. I'm not signing that contract.'

Slowly, annoyingly, he shook his head. 'I wasn't talking about the contract. I was talking about the fact that we want each other.'

'Not any more.' Emma curled her fingers, fighting the restless urge to reach out.

'Liar.' It was the merest whisper yet the accusation tolled through her body like a chiming bell.

He was right. That was the horrible truth.

Here in the intimate darkness, Emma felt the thousand proofs of it. The thrust of her pebbled nipples against the silk of her nightgown. The way that fine fabric grazed her bare flesh as if every nerve ending was suddenly too sensitive. The liquid heat between her legs. The edginess that made her want to shift and wriggle and, worse, press herself up against that hard body and discover how it would feel to…

'I don't want you, Christo.' It was the first bald-faced lie she could remember telling. But she refused to let him think she was so pathetic.

'Really?' He didn't sound at all dismayed. 'I could prove you wrong.' He shifted his weight, as if to step nearer, and Emma's heart leapt.

'No closer!' Emma flung her arm up, palm out. It took

everything she had to draw air into her lungs and find her voice but she did it. She'd learn to resist him if it killed her. 'I don't want to go to bed with you.'

Could he hear the lie?

At least he didn't move closer. In fact, to her astonishment, he turned and leaned his weight on the balustrade, looking out to sea. Her gaze roved his profile, from that strong nose to the hard angle of his jaw and up to the dark hair that looked rumpled, as if he'd dragged his hands through it.

Christo in a suit had been handsome. Christo pared back to basics and ever so slightly dishevelled made Emma's belly squeeze in longing.

Abruptly she turned away, sucking in a deep breath and placing her hands on the same railing.

'Don't look so scared. I told you I'd never force a woman. I'll wait till you come to me.'

She opened her mouth, to say that would never happen, then closed it again. The words would wash off him like water off a rock. She'd just have to demonstrate she meant what she said.

'So you don't want a contract now?' He sounded mildly curious, as if the issue of her sleeping with him was only of minor interest.

That, surely, would feed her determination? She'd never been brash or loud, demanding attention, but he'd already made her feel insignificant and taken for granted. She refused to settle for that.

'I don't want *that* contract.'

'Ah. But you still want everything else.'

'"Everything else" being property that's mine by right.' Adrenalin pumped through her blood. 'Or should have been if you hadn't inveigled your way into my grandfather's trust.'

How a wily businessman like Papou had been taken in

by Christo Karides, Emma would never understand. His health might have been failing but his mind had been sharp right till the end. It was he who'd warned her uncle that he'd over-extended, expanding his construction business so rapidly.

'Tell me about this place.' Christo's low voice drew her back to the present.

Instantly Emma stiffened as suspicion reared. 'Why do you want to know? I thought your company handled commercial property. Isn't that where you invest?'

'Relax. I only want to know because it's important to you. I heard it in your voice when you talked about it in Australia.' He paused. 'And you seem different here.'

She frowned. 'Different?'

'More assured. More confident.'

Emma shook her head and, standing straighter, turned to face her nemesis. 'I'm the same woman I always was. Nothing's changed.' Except she'd lost the last person she held dear. 'You were looking for a quiet mouse so you believed everything Papou told you about me.' Maybe *this* time he'd believe her.

'And your grandfather didn't get it right?' Instead of sounding annoyed, Christo's tone was merely curious.

She shrugged. 'He thought I was more delicate than I am.' Emma paused, wondering how much to share. But maybe this would convince Christo he was mistaken in thinking she could ever be the sort of wife he wanted. 'I had asthma badly as a kid and I was on the small side. Even though I grew out of the asthma, Papou never quite believed it. He was over-protective. He used to worry, so I learned not to confront him over things that didn't matter.'

Which had led to her taking the path of least resistance a lot of the time. Maybe if she'd stood up to him more often he wouldn't have persuaded Christo that she'd make the perfect homebody.

'I'm not a dutiful doormat.'

'So I've discovered.' Was that approval in his voice? She had to be imagining it. 'Now, about the villa…'

Emma stared up into that bold, shadowy face and wondered why he really wanted to know. On the other hand, talking with Christo was better than fighting him. Even with right on her side she found that unsettling.

She'd never enjoyed confrontation, but arguing with him was simultaneously frustrating and—Emma hated to admit it—exhilarating. As if the pulse of energy between them gave her a rush she'd never experienced before.

That was just plain crazy.

Finding her gaze straying down to those broad, straight shoulders and the muscled body limned by starlight, Emma swung away. She planted her palms on the railing and fixed her eyes on the view.

Which wasn't nearly as fascinating as the view of the man standing beside her.

She closed her eyes, willing herself to find the resolve she needed to pretend he didn't affect her.

Yet when she spoke her voice had a hoarse edge that she feared betrayed her. 'My grandparents met on Corfu. Papou had come back for a friend's wedding and my grandmother was on holiday from Australia. After a week, they were engaged. Three months later they were married.'

'Your grandfather was a decisive man.'

'Love at first sight is a family tradition. My aunt and uncle married after four months and my parents after two.' Emma snapped her mouth shut, belatedly seeing the connection to her own disastrous wedding. She'd fallen for Christo in record time. Because she genuinely believed in him, or because she'd been programmed to think love at first sight was utterly reasonable?

Now she knew to her cost how perilous that illusion was.

'And your grandfather owned this place?'

'It was his grandfather's.' She opened her eyes to survey the familiar coastline, the fragrant garden and behind it the silvery sweep of olive trees rising up the slope towards the hills. 'My grandmother adored it from the moment he brought her here. She was a horticulturalist and loved seeing what she could grow.'

'So they lived here.'

Emma shook her head. 'Only for a short time. Mainly they lived in Athens, then Australia. Papou was a businessman with interests on the mainland. In those days telecommuting wasn't an option. But this was always their favourite place. They'd come here several times a year. Even when they moved to Australia they came back regularly. We all did.'

'It had sentimental value, then.' He paused. 'For you too.'

Silently she nodded, surprised at the understanding in Christo's voice. She couldn't believe he had a sentimental bone in his body. Some of her happiest memories centred around this place. Of those precious years before her parents died. Of course there were other memories of them, of their day-to-day lives in Australia, but here at the villa there'd always been more time together as a family. Time Emma treasured.

She drew a breath and made herself focus on the present. 'It's a nice old place.' She wouldn't admit exactly how much it meant to her. Who knew how Christo would try to use that to his advantage? 'It's also an asset I can use to support myself.'

'Because you're determined to be independent.' His tone was non-committal but Emma heard the question.

'That's always been the plan.' Though she hadn't originally envisaged herself building a business here, in Greece. 'I've got a degree in business and event management. Plus experience in the field.' Okay, it was part-time experience, first with a major event organiser and later with a small but up-and-coming wedding planner. But full-time work had been impossible while she studied and looked after Papou. 'Of course I'll work.'

'Some would say marrying a wealthy man is a great career move. You need never lift a finger to support yourself.'

Emma's breath sucked in so sharply, pain shafted behind her ribs to radiate out and fill her chest.

She swivelled to face him, outrage obliterating caution. 'You...' She was so furious, the words backed up in her throat. In frustration she pointed a finger at his chest. 'You...'

Warm fingers enclosed hers and a thread of fire traced from his touch along to her elbow, then up to her shoulder, making her quiver.

'You're accusing me of marrying you for money?' Finally the words poured out, high and harsh.

'It's not unknown.' Christo's voice was matter-of-fact. His utter lack of expression was fuel to the fire of her anger. Did he think she'd been on the *make*?

'My family might not be as wealthy as yours, but we're not stony broke. At least, we weren't, before you weaselled your way into my grandfather's good graces.' For now Christo controlled her assets. 'But even if I didn't have a cent to my name—' scarily, she wasn't too far off that now '—I would never marry a man just to get his money.'

Vaguely Emma was aware of heat encasing her fingers as his big hand surrounded hers. But she was more concerned with convincing Christo he was utterly wrong about her.

'What proof have you got?' His tone was infuriatingly calm. 'Women do it all the time.'

That, Emma realised with a jolt, was the second time he'd referred to women cold-bloodedly targeting men as meal tickets. Suddenly she had a glimpse of the down side of being a mega-wealthy bachelor. Christo would never know how much of his appeal was down to his bank balance.

Tough! That didn't give him the right to use her for his convenience. Or accuse her of being a liar.

'Well, I don't. *I* didn't come looking for *you*, Christo Karides. *I* didn't deliberately set out to con you into marriage.' That had been him, targeting her and playing up to her hopes and vulnerabilities.

'So, if you didn't marry me for my money…' his words were slow and warm, like sun-drenched honey dropping onto her skin '…why *did* you marry me, Emma?'

It was only as the darkness pulsed between them and the silence grew heavy with waiting that Emma recognised his trap. To tell the truth meant admitting that she'd fallen in love with him. Or at least fallen for the mirage of love.

'This conversation's getting us nowhere. That's in the past and—'

'On the contrary, this conversation is just getting interesting.' He lowered his head, as if trying to read her face in the darkness. 'Tell me why you married me, Emma.'

That voice, honey now mixed with rumbling gravel, scraped through her insides. But, instead of leaving painful grazes, it stirred something altogether unwanted. Something she needed to banish. If only she knew how!

Suddenly she realised the danger of being this close to him. Of his flesh on hers. 'I want to go inside.'

'Could it be,' he went on as if she hadn't spoken, 'Because of *this*…?'

He tugged her hand, pulling her against him. Emma's hissed breath was loud as she planted her other palm on his chest to push him away.

But before she could he'd raised her captured hand to his face and pressed his lips to her palm. She felt surprisingly soft lips and the delicious abrasion of his hair-roughened jaw, a reminder of his masculinity, as if she needed it!

Instantly sensation juddered through her.

Desire.

Delight.

Weakness.

Shivers reverberated through her and Emma knew she had to fight this. But then Christo moved, bending lower to kiss the sensitive flesh of her wrist, creating a shower of sparks in her blood.

The trouble was Emma had so little experience. There'd been a guy at university when she'd been eighteen but that had never progressed beyond a few kisses, because her grandmother had died and suddenly, more than ever, she'd been needed at home. She had no experience withstanding such powerfully erotic caresses. Or the demands of her own body, finally woken after so long.

Firming her mouth, she pushed that unyielding chest with her free hand. It made no impact.

Or perhaps she didn't push very hard. For now Christo was kissing his way along the bare flesh of her forearm where the wide sleeve of her robe fell back.

His grip wasn't tight. She could yank her hand free. If only she could find the willpower to do it.

But, oh, the lush sensations spreading from those tiny yet incredibly intimate kisses.

Her breath sawed and in her ears blood rushed helter-skelter.

He'd reached her elbow and she stiffened like a yacht's sail snapping taut in the wind. Taut but trembling too, at the sensations he evoked. Her hand on his chest no longer pushed. Instead it splayed, fingers wide, absorbing the sultry heat of his hard chest and the teasing friction of the smudge of dark hair on his pectorals.

'Stop that now.' Because, heaven help her, she couldn't. 'I'm not sleeping with you, Christo.'

That caught his attention. He looked up and even in the

gloom she caught the brilliance of his eyes as he looked down at her. Then, without uttering a word, he put his mouth to her arm and slowly licked her inner elbow.

Emma's knees all but gave way as a frighteningly potent shot of lust punched her. She made a sound, a soft, keening noise that she wouldn't have thought possible if she hadn't heard it slide from her lips.

She cleared her throat, ready to demand he release her, when she felt the scrape of teeth nipping the soft flesh in the crease of her elbow. Then almost immediately the strong draw against her skin as he sucked the spot.

Emma bit down hard on her lip to prevent a groan escaping into the night. She'd had no idea something as ordinary as an elbow could be so sensitive. That it could make her feel...

Ready for sex. That was how she felt. With her trembling limbs and that pulsing point down between her thighs that urged her to move closer to Christo. There was an aching hollowness inside and her breasts seemed fuller than before, eager for contact, her nipples impossibly hard. If she followed that animal instinct she would rub herself against him, purring and pleading for follow through.

Her own weakness terrified her.

'I said I don't want to go to bed with you.' Her voice was too loud and too wobbly.

For answer he released her hand which wavered uselessly in the air then slowly dropped to her side. Instead of moving back he stroked his fingertips over her cheek. All she had to do was pull her head back a couple of centimetres to sever the contact but she couldn't do it. Instead she stood as if mesmerised by the caress of long, hard fingers that worked magic with each touch.

'I don't believe you.'

Why should he?

That was what terrified her. Not Christo's practised seduction but the fact that, after all he'd done, she still had no defences against him, or more precisely against her wilful body's craving for satisfaction.

The breath shuddered through her lungs. She felt herself sway, but managed to pull back at the last moment.

Christo followed.

Emma felt his warm breath on her cheek, the heat of his frame close to hers. She dragged in that leather, wood and male spice scent that made something inside her fizz like champagne bubbles.

Then those warm lips brushed her jaw. So lightly she almost wondered if she'd imagined it. But there was no mistaking the scorching trail of heat curling from her chin to her ear and then along to her mouth.

Emma had stopped breathing, stopped thinking. Her hands pressed to Christo's bare body which was part of the spell he wove. His smooth flesh and springy muscle invited exploration.

He kissed his way to the corner of her mouth then paused, hovering half a breath away.

Her lips tingled with want as she waited for him to kiss her properly. Not as he'd kissed her in the church, just a brief salutation to satisfy custom. Not as he'd kissed her when they'd got engaged, tenderly but too short and too chaste.

What Emma wanted, what she craved, was full-blown passion. She wanted to fall into that whirlwind of rapture she'd read about, and that her body assured her was waiting for her if she'd just let go and give herself to Christo.

She might detest him but she had no doubt he could allay the terrible gnawing hunger inside. The hunger *he'd* created. All she had to do was…

'Say it, Emma. Invite me into your bed. You're aching for me. I'll make it good for you.'

Of course he would.

But then, afterwards, what about her self-respect?

How could she hold her head up?

She'd let this man sweep her off her feet into a hazy romantic cloud that had about as much link to reality as unicorns prancing along the white sand of the beach below.

Seconds later Emma found herself in the doorway to her room, hands braced as if to stop herself reaching for Christo. She couldn't remember telling herself to step back. It must have been some primal survival instinct so deeply buried as to be almost automatic.

For there was no doubt now that Christo was the most dangerous man she'd ever met. He wasn't just cunning and ruthless, he'd introduced her to desire, and now her frustrated body had imprinted on him as the one man who could satisfy her.

It was ludicrous and appalling.

It scared her witless.

She grabbed the handle of the French door.

'I don't want you. I'll never want you.'

He stood, arms folded, watching as she tugged the door closed. In the instant before it snicked shut, she heard his voice, soft, deep and, oh, so sure.

'We both know that's a lie, Emma. But take your time. When we finally have sex it will be worth the wait.'

CHAPTER SEVEN

CHRISTO PULLED HARD through the water, forcing his body to the limit in an effort to weary himself. Anything to douse the frustration that had him wound so tight.

How had he ever thought winning Emma over would be simple? She had more determination, more sheer obstinacy, than any negotiator he'd ever confronted.

Her insistence on resisting him, despite the fact she clearly wanted him, was infuriating. He told himself if it weren't for the fact he was committed to her he'd walk away.

Christo had given her more than he'd ever given any woman. His name, his word, his promise for the future. Yet she looked at him with those glittering hazel eyes as if he were the devil incarnate.

Christo gritted his teeth and quickened his stroke till his shoulders and legs ached and his lungs were ready to burst.

Treading water, he hauled in a needy gulp of air and turned. In the distance the villa nestled into the curve of the bay, gracious and charming.

He'd thought Emma was just like that too, a mix of gentle ways and unobtrusive prettiness. An easy fit for his needs.

His harsh laugh echoed across the water.

Easy!

Anyone less easy he had yet to meet.

Oh, she certainly did her best to avoid direct confrontation. These last three weekends, whenever he'd arrived from Athens, she'd been the perfect hostess.

Christo ground his teeth. It was true he'd wanted a woman who could do him proud when entertaining, but it was something far more personal he wanted from her.

Far more personal. Despite the cool water and his fatigue after the sprint swim, he still felt that frustration low in his body.

Three weeks! He couldn't believe she'd held out for three weeks. He'd thought she'd break by now. For, try as she might, she couldn't hide her desire for him.

That first night here he'd almost had her in his arms and in his bed. She'd been like a fragrant summer rosebud, unfurling into his hand, velvet-soft and exquisite. His groin throbbed at the memory. But his little bride had an unexpectedly thorny resolve. Besides, he'd given his word. He'd promised to wait till she was ready.

The taut weight in his lower body testified to the toll his self-imposed patience was taking on him.

At least in one area she'd lived up to expectations. Her relationship with Anthea. Whenever he saw them together the brittle aura of containment around his niece chipped a little more. As for Emma, her policy of not getting involved had lasted about two seconds. Increasingly Anthea turned to Emma rather than the nanny paid to care for her.

Despite her obstinacy, Emma had a soft side. She was ruled by emotions. Plus she suffered from the same sexual frustration he did.

Christo's mouth curled up. All he had to do was take advantage of the opportunities that arose. Ignore his pride and chagrin that she hadn't already come to him and *make* those opportunities happen. Remind her again of the unfulfilled desire sizzling between them.

He lowered his head and began a steady overarm stroke towards the shore.

Half an hour later, a towel slung over his shoulder and his body warm from the sun, he strolled up the path from the cove and through the garden. A fat bee droned in the sunshine and the smell of roses caught his nostrils.

The irony of it didn't escape him. The drowsing villa

with its secluded garden and scented roses might have been Sleeping Beauty's bower. Somewhere inside was Emma, his bride, waiting to be woken by his touch.

She'd never admitted it but he suspected she was a virgin. Those tell-tale blushes and the slight clumsiness of her kisses had raised his suspicions. Which was one of the reasons he hadn't pressed her too hard.

Once they were lovers, once they'd shared intimate physical pleasure, he knew there'd be no more holding back.

He rounded a corner and stopped. It seemed his imagination was more accurate than he'd suspected. For there was Sleeping Beauty herself.

Emma lay fast asleep on a sun lounger.

His gaze tracked her from her honey-toned hair splayed around her shoulders to her bare feet. Afternoon sun gilded her toned legs where her lacy white skirt rucked up high above her knees. Christo's pulse quickened and his throat dried as he imagined exploring that satiny skin.

With each gentle breath her breasts swelled up against the vivid red of her sleeveless top, riveting his attention.

Even in sleep she was more striking than she'd been in Australia.

Because of her bright clothes? Or because he'd begun to appreciate she was far more than the docile bride he'd assumed?

A couple of children's books were tumbled across her lap, making her look as if she hadn't intended to fall asleep.

That was when he saw movement beside her and stiffened. At the same moment little Anthea, who'd been sitting on the flagstones half-hidden by the sun lounger, looked up.

Big brown eyes met his and Christo felt again that stifling sensation in his chest. It was as if the years scrolled back and he was looking into the wary eyes of his new stepsister, Cassie. Cassie had been older, almost a teenager, yet those eyes were the same. And so was the suffocating shadow of guilt that chilled his belly.

He hadn't been able to help Cassie all those years ago. In fact his casual attempt at kindness to the nervous little girl had backfired spectacularly. Because of him her whole future had been blighted. Was it any wonder he found it difficult being with Anthea? She might be tiny, but she was so like Cassie he couldn't look at her without remembering.

Christo waited for Anthea to turn away as she usually did. Proof again that he'd done the right thing organising a new mother and a nanny to care for her, since patently he wasn't cut out for it.

To his surprise, instead of shrinking back, his step-niece took her time frowning down at something she held then looked up at him again. Her eyes were bright and her look trembled between excited and tentative. As if she wanted to share with him but was afraid of being rebuffed.

Slowly she lifted a large piece of paper for him to see. It was covered in green crayon scrawls.

Christo felt something give deep in his chest, like a knot suddenly loosening, cutting the tension that stiffened his body. His breath drifted out, making him realise he'd been holding it.

He told himself he should leave her be, simply walk away. For he knew, even if she didn't, that he wasn't the person she needed.

But her expression, turning now from expectation to disappointment at his lack of response, slashed through his caution.

How could he resist?

He padded barefoot across the warm flagstones to Anthea. Her brow wrinkled in concentration as she tilted her head up to look at him.

Christo's heart gave an unsteady thump. How his business competitors would laugh if they could see him now, scared of a little girl, or more precisely of somehow doing the wrong thing for her. He didn't know children. He had virtually no experience of them. And the one time he'd actually bonded with one it had ended in disaster.

Breathing deep through his nostrils, he hunkered down before her. It was a relief to look away from that intense brown stare and focus on her drawing.

Amongst the swirl of circles he discovered four downward strokes that might have been legs. 'You drew this?' he said, buying time. He still hadn't a clue what it was.

Gravely Anthea nodded, watching expectantly.

Christo frowned, his brain racing. Clearly she expected more.

'It's very good.' Did he sound as stilted as he feared?

'Nice dat.' They were the first words Anthea had spoken directly to him and he should have celebrated this sign of thawing, except he had no idea what she meant.

Till she lifted one dimpled hand and pointed. 'Dat.'

Christo followed her hand and saw a white cat stretched out in the shade of a tree, one ear twitching, as if following their conversation. He looked back at the drawing and enlightenment dawned. There, he spied two triangles that might have been feline ears and a curling line that could be a tail.

'You drew the cat?'

She nodded emphatically.

'Do you like cats?'

Another nod.

Now what? Clearly he was meant to contribute more.

Briefly Christo thought of the work he could be doing, the calls he should make. Of waking Emma or rousting out Anthea's nanny to take over.

Was he really so craven?

'Would you like me to draw a cat for you?' He wasn't consciously aware of forming the words but suddenly they were out and she was nodding again, a hint of a smile curving her mouth. Warmth trickled through Christo's chest.

He settled more comfortably on the flagstones and took the drawing she held out. But, instead of turning it over and drawing on the back of it, he chose a purple crayon from those scattered nearby and wrote her name on one corner, sounding out the letters as he went.

'There, now everyone will know it's yours.'

Fascinated, Anthea traced the letters with her finger, one dark plait falling forward and brushing his arm. It seemed she'd forgotten to be wary of him.

'Now you.' She pointed to the blank pages nearby. 'A dat.'

Once more Christo was rocked by a moment of déjà vu. It had been years since he'd drawn. Since that weekend when he'd amused his shy young stepsister with sketches and cartoons to make her smile. In those days drawing—or doodling, as his father had scathingly called it—had been a habit. A hobby that had distracted him from the pressures of his father's demands and their uncomfortable family life.

But not after that weekend.

Christo swallowed the sour tang of bile as old memories stirred. Setting his jaw, he shoved all that aside. It was over, dead and buried.

He took a sheet, glanced at the cat, now sitting up watching them, and began to draw.

At his side, Anthea watched, apparently entranced, as a few swift lines became a cat half-asleep in the sun. Another couple of lines and the cat was dozing over a book that looked rather like the picture book beside Anthea's stack of crayons.

Christo heard a childish giggle and added a striped sun umbrella similar to the one behind Emma. Anthea giggled again but shook her head when he went to give it to her.

'Put your name.'

This conversation was the most she'd ever said to him

and it felt like a victory. Not that he had any illusions about ever being particularly close to Anthea. She'd already bonded with Emma and that relationship would strengthen with time.

Christo would provide a comfortable home, protection and support, but as for being a close father figure... He shook his head even as he wrote his name in clear letters for Anthea.

He'd never known love from either of his parents. To one he'd been a convenience and to the other something to be moulded into the perfect heir to the Karides commercial empire. The heir to a man who married trophy wives and expected his son to be as ruthless and successful as he.

Christo's lips twisted in a shadow of a smile as he thought how proud the old man would be if he were still alive. For Christo was far more successful than his father had ever been, having expanded the family business to a completely new level. As for ruthless—he'd always tried to be more humanitarian than his father. But when the pressure was on, when he really needed something, like a mother for Anthea, it turned out he was every bit as unrelenting as the old man.

The knowledge was a cold, hard lump in his belly.

He ignored it, for there was no point pining over things that could never change. Instead he leaned over the paper and concentrated on a new drawing for his eager audience.

Emma drifted out of her doze to the sound of Anthea's excited voice. She heard another voice answer, a deep, reassuring blur of sound that soothed her back towards slumber.

Blearily Emma tried to summon the strength to move, fighting the fog that enveloped her. She never napped during the day but last night, knowing Christo was in the room next to hers, she'd been unable to sleep.

It was like that each weekend when he returned to the island. In the beginning she'd wondered if he'd break his word, try to 'persuade' her into his bed. But as the days and nights had passed and he'd kept his word that fear had subsided.

Yet she was still on tenterhooks.

Because it's not Christo you're afraid of.

It was herself. She hadn't yet been able to banish that simmering attraction she felt. The physical awareness whenever he was near. For, despite his promise to wait, Christo was often near, not crowding her or touching her, but *close*. She'd feel his stare and look up to discover she had little defence against the heat in his eyes. Inevitably answering need flared.

She told herself again and again he didn't really want *her*, except as a convenient child minder. But her besotted self, the one who'd once tumbled headlong into the romantic mirage he'd created, refused to listen.

Finally she forced her eyelids open to squint at the sunlight. She moved and the books on her lap slid sideways. Panic stirred. Anthea. Was she okay? Emma was supposed to be minding her while the nanny had her afternoon off.

'Dog now. *Pease*.'

Emma turned towards the little girl's voice and would have fallen off the lounge if she hadn't been lying down.

For there was big, bad Christo Karides, down on the pavement with his niece.

Emma blinked and rubbed her eyes, wondering if this was some hard-to-shake dream. But the image remained. The little girl in her shorts and T-shirt, looking up earnestly at the man beside her.

Christo Karides in nothing but damp, black swim shorts and acres of bare, muscled body, was spectacular. A shot of adrenalin hit Emma's blood, making her heart kick into a frantic rhythm. Ever since the night on her balcony she'd been haunted by thoughts of his body. But he looked even more impossibly delicious in broad daylight.

It struck her that for the first time he didn't wear the closed expression that usually clamped his features when he was around Anthea. He seemed at ease.

Almost. He leaned over a sheet of paper, his brow furrowed in concentration, his expression intent.

Moving slowly, not wanting to draw his attention, Emma sat higher to get a better view. What she saw held her spellbound. Using a crayon, Christo deftly sketched a couple of lines that turned into a whiskery, canine face wearing an almost comical expression of longing. A few more sure strokes and a body emerged with short legs and a curling tail. Finally he completed the picture by adding a large bone, almost as big as the dog, which explained the animal's hungry look.

He was good. Very good. The dog had such character, she could imagine it trotting around the corner of the villa, dragging that oversized bone with it.

Anthea laughed with delight, the sound as bright as sunshine. Emma's lips curved in response. The little girl was gradually relaxing here in Corfu and smiled more often. But she was still withdrawn and shy. Hearing her so exuberant was wonderful.

Emma shafted a curious glance back to Christo.

For once he wasn't aware of her scrutiny, focused instead on the girl beside him.

'More!' Anthea was so excited she knelt beside him, her tiny hands on one muscled knee as she leaned over to look at the drawing.

'Why don't you draw a friend for the dog?' He pushed the paper towards her and held out the crayon.

After a moment's consideration she nodded, her small fingers plucking the crayon from his broad palm.

Emma's chest squeezed at the sight of them together. It

wasn't that she was eager for a baby, but she *had* imagined Christo as the father of her children some time in the future. Had imagined those powerful arms cradling their baby.

Seeing him now, gentle and patient as Anthea scribbled what looked like a woolly sheep across the rest of the page, Emma couldn't prevent a pang of loss. Silly to pine for a man who wasn't real. The Christo Karides she'd fallen for was a façade, deliberately constructed to gull her into marriage.

Yet, watching her husband, she couldn't help mourning the loss of what might have been. If only Christo had been genuine.

'Tell me about what you've drawn,' Christo murmured.

''Nother dog. See?' Anthea leaned in, the tip of her tongue showing between her teeth as she added another figure, this time with an oversized head and stick legs. 'And me.' Another lop-sided figure appeared. 'And you.'

She sat back, beaming, and Emma had a perfect view of Christo. His face changed, an expression of surprise and pleasure making him look years younger than thirty-one. It made her realise how often he looked older than he was—still devastatingly attractive, but as if he carried an unseen burden that kept him too serious. That was, she supposed, what came of running a successful multinational company.

Then he seemed to collect himself. 'Wonderful! Should we put in anything else?' He looked across the terrace to where Dora's old cat watched them.

'Emma!' Anthea leaned across Christo, chose a blue crayon and held it up. 'Put in Emma.'

At the little girl's words, he lifted his head, his gaze colliding with Emma's.

This time the impact wasn't so much a sizzle as an immediate burst of ignition. Emma felt it like a whoosh of flame exploding deep in her belly.

But now there was more too. For Anthea followed his

gaze and saw her awake. Immediately she grabbed the picture and brought it over, excitedly pointing out the dog and identifying the figures she'd added. As Emma smiled, nodded and praised the little girl, her gaze met Christo's in a shared look of understanding and pleasure. A mutual relief that Anthea was starting to come out of her shell.

Perhaps it was crazy, but to Emma it felt like a rare, precious moment of connection.

As if, for once, she and Christo were on the same side. As if their shared purpose in providing for Anthea drew them together.

As if they weren't really enemies.

Except thinking like that had got her into this mess in the first place.

The spell was broken as Anthea held out the paper to him. After a moment he took it. But, instead of adding another figure to the crowded page, he turned it over.

She watched, fascinated, as he began to draw. Random lines coalesced and separated. Shapes appeared, familiar features. When he was done Anthea clapped her hands.

'Nice Emma.' The little girl crooned the words and held the page up.

It was a remarkable piece, considering it was executed with a thick child's crayon on cheap paper. Christo really was talented. But what held Emma's attention was the unexpected beauty of what he'd drawn. Not merely that the portrait was well-executed and recognisable as her. But that, for the first time in her life, Emma *looked* beautiful.

Her brow crinkled. What had he done to make her appear different? It looked so like her and yet on the page she was…more.

'Beautiful Emma.' His words feathered across her bare arms and wound themselves down her spine.

'Hardly.' She lifted her eyes to his, angling her chin. 'There's no need to exaggerate.'

He didn't so much as blink. 'I never exaggerate.'

No. He just implied more than was true. Such as making out he cared for her to get her to agree to marry him.

Swinging her legs over the side of the lounger, Emma got up, belatedly catching the spill of Anthea's books.

'It's a lovely picture, Anthea, but I like the one you drew better. Perhaps you could make another one for me to keep while I go inside and work? I'm sure Christo would love to help you.'

She didn't even look at him, just waited to see Anthea happily settled down with another sheet of paper, then turned on her heel and headed indoors.

Christo could look after his niece for once. Emma needed to work on her plans if she was ever going to turn the villa into a viable business.

But it wasn't business on her mind as she walked away. It was that strange moment of connection she and Christo had shared over Anthea's head. The instance of common purpose and understanding. It had felt profound. Even now Emma felt its echo tremble through her, making her skin shiver and her insides warm.

Or perhaps, more dangerously, it was a reaction to Christo's assessing stare that she felt trawl down her body as she walked.

She told herself she imagined it, yet her step quickened. She needed to get inside. Away from the temptation to turn back and see if she'd imagined the spark of something new in Christo's eyes.

To Emma's surprise, he stayed with Anthea for the next hour. Whatever had held the little girl back from him earlier had vanished. Whenever Emma looked out—and, to her chagrin, that was often—the pair had their heads together, poring over drawings then Anthea's books.

She heard the deep murmur of Christo's voice, a rich

velvet counterpoint to Anthea's higher voice, and satisfaction stirred. In the couple of weeks Anthea had been
there, Emma had grown fond of the girl. It was good to
think that she was beginning to build a relationship with
her only relative.

Curiosity stirred about that family. Emma sensed there
was more to their story than the death of Anthea's mother.
She recalled the dark edge to Christo's voice as he'd talked
of his stepsister and couldn't douse her desire to know more.

Desire. There it was again. That word summed up too
many of her feelings for Christo.

'Emma?' She jerked round to find the man himself in
the doorway, still almost naked in black swim shorts. Why
didn't he put on some clothes? Emma hated the way her
heartbeat revved at the sight of all that bare, masculine
flesh.

She looked past him but saw no sign of Anthea. Instantly she was on alert, hyperaware that her visceral response to him made her vulnerable. Emma tried to spend
as little time as possible alone with Christo but somehow
that never quite worked.

'Anthea is with Dora, having a snack.'

Had he read her nerves? The thought was intolerable.
Emma got up from the desk where she'd been working on
her business plan but Christo was already padding across
the room towards her.

'We need to talk.'

Her brow pinched. His tone and his watchful expression
told her she wasn't going to like this.

'About Anthea?' A couple of weeks ago her thoughts
would have gone instantly to their tenuous marriage arrangement. Strange how even the outrageous could seem
almost normal after a while.

'No.' He paused and she sensed he marshalled his words
carefully. The idea sent a premonition of trouble skitter-

ing through her. 'About our marriage. The paparazzi has got hold of the story.'

Surely he'd been prepared for that? Christo had insisted on fencing the estate with high-tech security infrastructure to keep out trespassers. He'd been convinced news of their very private wedding would score media attention. When she'd protested he'd spoken of protecting her and Anthea, which had ended her arguments. The little girl had been through enough without being hunted by the press.

'Is that all? It had to happen some time.' The tension pinching Emma's shoulders eased.

Christo stopped so close, she saw herself in his eyes. She hitched a silent breath and shoved her hands into the pockets of her skirt.

'Unfortunately it's not just the wedding they know about. There are reports that you ran away before the honeymoon and that we've separated.'

Storm-dark eyes bored into her and Emma realised Christo had just received this news. The last three weeks he'd been annoyingly at ease while she'd fretted about their impossible relationship. Now he hadn't had time to bury his anger under a façade of calm.

'It's close enough to the truth.'

His mouth tightened. '*Not* the story we're going to give them.'

Emma frowned. 'Do we have to give them any story? Surely you don't have to comment? You're Christo Karides. I thought you were above worrying about gossip.'

'I will *not* be pilloried in public as a deserted husband, or as some sort of Bluebeard who frightened off his bride.'

Even if you did?

The words danced on Emma's tongue but she didn't say them. She read his implacable expression and knew there was no point saying it. It would only inflame the situation.

Papou had taught her that no Greek male worth his salt

would allow a slight to his masculinity. Being seen as an undesirable husband clearly fitted under that heading.

'You'll need to start wearing your rings.' His gaze dropped to her bare left hand.

Emma froze on the spot, remembering the day she'd last worn them. Her wedding day.

'That's not necessary. Besides,' she hurried on when he opened his mouth to speak, 'I can't. I left them in Melbourne.' She'd dragged off the dainty gold band and the enormous solitaire diamond and left them with Steph for safekeeping. The memory of that moment of disillusionment and despair left a rancid taste in her mouth.

Christo's eyes narrowed but instead of berating her he merely paused. 'They can be replaced.'

Which proved just how little those symbols of their vows to each other meant to him.

Emma swallowed, hating the scratchy sensation as her throat closed convulsively.

'Me wearing a wedding ring won't be enough to convince anyone all's well with our marriage.'

'Of course not.'

The look of calculation on his face made her nervous. Emma crossed her arms.

'So how are you going to convince everyone?'

Christo's mouth curled up in a slow smile that simultaneously set her hormones jangling and sent a cold chill across her nape.

'Not me. *We*.' He paused, watching her reaction. 'You're coming with me to Athens this week. Together we're going to present a united front as a pair of deliriously happy newlyweds.'

As Christo's words sank in, Emma realised two things. That he was utterly serious. And that it wasn't just determination she read in his face—it was anticipation.

CHAPTER EIGHT

EMMA PROTESTED. SHE flat out refused to go.

But Christo was as immovable as Mount Pantokrator looming imperiously over the island. He refused to countenance her refusal.

She'd been ready to fight him over his need to appear macho and perfect. The adoring public saw him as a shining light in difficult economic times, a beacon of hope for the future. Frankly she'd enjoy seeing him taken down a peg.

But to her chagrin he cut off her arguments quickly. His character and status were inseparable from the success of his company. Especially now he'd turned from his usual international focus to concentrate on a major redevelopment in Athens. Persuading investors to come in with him was tough when Greece still suffered hard economic times, but he was determined to contribute to a resurgence.

If it came out that she'd run from him, the scandal could undermine confidence in his character and decision-making. His business would be affected. So would the livelihoods of his employees and contractors. As would others who relied on his continued success. Like her uncle.

But if they gave the paparazzi opportunities to see them as a couple the press would soon shift to other stories.

The prospect of being hounded wherever she went chilled her blood. And Anthea would be caught in the media circus too. It was in everyone's interest to minimise gossip.

Which was how Emma found herself staring across the Athens skyline from Christo's penthouse. The silhouette of the Acropolis was reassuringly familiar, as was the distant bright metal shimmer of the sea in the early evening light.

Yet Christo's Athens bore little resemblance to hers.

First there'd been the private jet. Then the discreet security detail. Emma had been prepared for the plush limousine, but not to have it waved through a stationary traffic snarl by a policeman who'd all but saluted as they'd passed. Then the no-expenses-spared shopping trip which had made Emma's eyes bulge.

Now this. The expansive sitting room seemed all glass and marble against that multi-million-dollar backdrop.

Emma had been into luxurious homes, assisting with lavish celebrations. She knew quality, and this was it.

Everything spoke of wealth, but not ostentatiously. No over-gilded ornamentation or fussiness here. Just the best of the best, from the soft furnishings to the custom-made furniture and original art.

She wandered through the room, past a modern fireplace which was in itself a work of art, to stop before a wall hanging that turned out to be a traditionally woven rug in deep crimson and jewel colours. The richness of its tones and tactile weave drew her hand. But she didn't touch. It was probably worth a fortune.

Emma's pulse skipped. Speaking of fortunes...

The hand she'd raised dropped to the delicate fabric of her dress. She'd never worn a designer original.

Involuntarily her gaze darted to the mirror above the fireplace. A stranger looked back.

The sheen of dark green silk accentuated the dress's close fit. Emma blinked. The change wasn't just that, or her newly styled hair. Nor the prohibitively expensive shoes.

She tilted her head. Was it the subtle smokiness of her new eye make-up? Or the lustre of the almost nude lipstick she'd never have chosen on her own?

When Christo had mentioned shopping for clothes, Emma had wanted to refuse anything bought with his funds.

But she knew the importance of appearances. The casual

clothes she'd packed for her honeymoon would look rustic in a sophisticated city venue. She wanted to scotch the stories about their mismatched marriage, not add to them.

Yet she'd resented being foisted on a cousin of Damen, Christo's best friend, whom Christo had lined up to take her shopping. But for once her husband had been right. She'd needed someone like Clio, with an eye for fashion and experience navigating Athens' most exclusive boutiques.

To Emma's surprise the other woman, despite her dauntingly glamorous appearance, had proved to have an irreverent sense of humour, a warm heart plus an unerring eye. She...

Her thoughts skittered to a halt as footsteps sounded from the corridor. Firm, masculine footsteps.

Everything inside Emma stilled, except her fluttery pulse that beat shallow and fast, like a moth trapped against glass. She spun round, lifting her chin.

Christo was a tall figure in the shadows at the far edge of the room, his expression unreadable. Was it a trick of the light that made that firm jaw look tense?

The air surged with sudden energy, like a giant heartbeat. She felt her nerves quicken, waiting.

Till she realised this was all her reaction to Christo. Freshly shaven and wearing a made-to-measure tuxedo, he looked good enough to eat. Her mouth dried as her imagination detoured in that direction and she forced herself to concentrate.

Did he like what he saw?

Furiously she told herself it didn't matter whether he did or not. While she wouldn't adopt this look every day, *she* liked it. That was what mattered. And that she looked sophisticated enough to pass as the wife of Greece's sexiest billionaire.

Christo had refused to be made a laughing stock in public. But how much worse for her to be the woman everyone knew he'd married for convenience, not love?

The thought sent a judder of revulsion through her. Come hell or high water, she'd play her part in this masquerade. She refused to be a figure of pity.

Still Christo said nothing. That brooding silence got on her nerves.

She turned towards the lounge where she'd put the wispy wrap and tiny evening bag that matched her jewelled green shoes. 'Are you ready to go?'

'Unless you want a drink to fortify yourself?' Out of her peripheral vision she saw him step into the room.

'I'd rather have a clear head, thank you.' Emma felt the familiar knife-twist of pain in her middle. The pang of hurt that even now she couldn't kill her attraction to him.

'I have something for you.'

Emma turned sharply, alerted by a note of something she hadn't heard before in Christo's voice. She couldn't place it.

But she did recognise the flare of heat in those dark blue-grey eyes. A thrill shot past her guard to resonate deep within her core. Her fingers curled into her purse, digging like talons into the fragile silk.

'A gift?' Emma strove for an insouciant tone. She already wore a new wedding band and a stunning gold filigree and diamond engagement ring. The latter was beautiful but felt like a brand of ownership. 'Not divorce papers, by any chance?'

One coal black eyebrow rose in a look that should have been annoyingly superior but, in her flustered state, seemed appallingly sexy.

Emma shut her eyes, praying for strength. This physical infatuation was supposed to disintegrate the longer she was exposed to him, not intensify.

'Emma?' The low burr of his voice rippled to her womb.

Opening her eyes, she fixed her gaze near his bow tie. But that was a mistake because above it was that oh-so-masculine jaw and stern chin with just a hint of an intriguing cleft.

'Are you all right?'

Surprised at his concern, Emma jerked her eyes up to his. A mistake, for she was instantly captured by a steely stare that this time seemed softer, like dawn mist over mountains.

'Of course. Why wouldn't I be?'

Christo read doubt behind the defiance in her fine eyes and felt protectiveness stir. He knew how tough it could be to maintain a smiling façade when in private all was turmoil. But he'd had a lifetime to master the art. He'd plucked Emma from the shelter of her home and thrust her into his world. He owed her his support.

'How about a truce for tonight? I'll keep the wolves at bay. All you need to do is smile and follow my lead. I'll look after you.'

Her head tilted to one side. 'That's supposed to make me feel better?'

It was a cheap jibe that should have annoyed him. Yet, like the crack about divorce papers, it had the opposite effect. Christo could weather a little snarkiness and he'd developed an appreciation for Emma's resilience.

Once he'd thought he wanted a quiet, docile wife. Now he discovered he preferred spirit to automatic obedience. Emma's eyes blazed brilliantly and he was pleased to see there was colour in her cheeks.

When he'd walked in, she'd looked pale. Beautiful, surprisingly so, but a cool stranger.

Even now he was unsettled by that first impression of her, standing like a glamorous stranger in his home. She'd looked sexy, svelte and sophisticated in the strapless fitted dress. He'd known in that instant she'd be accepted without question by his acquaintances and the press, for she had the appearance of so many other women in that milieu. Glossy. Confident. Gorgeous.

Strangely, that knowledge was undercut by disappointment. Even concern. That the Emma he'd begun to discover on Corfu had disappeared.

Tonight was about public perception, yet Christo hated the idea of the real Emma being lost or transformed into just another glamorous socialite.

'I may not be Prince Charming, but this time you can rely on me. I promise.'

Her gaze snagged on his and something beat hard in his belly. Something more than sexual desire or anticipation about tonight's performance.

Christo's breath frayed as he read her expression, saw defiance and annoyance and—could it be yearning?

Abruptly she turned away, as if to leave. 'Well, I can't promise this Cinderella won't turn into a pumpkin at midnight, but I'll do my best.'

Relief buzzed through him. Any fear that Emma had been subsumed by her new, sophisticated look died at her words.

'Wait. Don't you want your gift?'

'Gift?' She was half-turned away, but he saw her frown.

'For tonight. I want you to shine.' He withdrew a flat box and held it out to her.

Weird that he actually felt nervous, giving Emma jewellery. As if he hadn't given girlfriends jewellery before. Only this time it felt imperative that he got it right.

Maybe he was still smarting over the perfunctory glance she'd given the new rings he'd ordered. As if the exquisite filigree work, modelled on ancient designs and studded with flawless diamonds, hadn't impressed her in the slightest.

Annoyance flared. Christo wasn't used to questioning his emotions. He held out the leather box and flipped the lid open.

His anger died at Emma's long sigh of appreciation.

'I've never seen anything like it. What sort of stones are they?'

'Tourmaline.' The dark green was richer than emeralds, in his opinion. As soon as Clio had called him to describe Emma's dress, he'd known what he wanted. Finding it had been another matter. This set had just been flown into Athens for him.

'They're stunning. But I don't wear much jewellery. I don't want to look—'

'You'll look perfect,' Christo urged. Why wasn't he surprised that Emma, of all the women he'd known, should hesitate to accept beautiful jewels? 'Everyone will expect you to wear something spectacular. I'm supposed to be doting on you, remember?'

He watched as his words had their inevitable effect, cutting through her hesitation and stiffening her spine. For a second he regretted the loss of that misty smile of wonder on Emma's face. But, as she put on the long tourmaline and diamond eardrops, he was too busy maintaining his expression of gentle teasing when everything inside turned hot and urgent.

The elegant Art Deco style earrings swung against her slender throat. The colour intensified the green in her hazel eyes, making them glow.

Or was that something else in her expression?

Need pulsed through him. Not the need to put an end to public gossip, but the need to haul his pretty wife close and bury his face in the scented hollow of her pale throat. To smash down the barriers between them and make love to her.

'Now the necklace.' His voice hit a gravelly note.

'No.' She shook her head. 'It would be too much. On some other woman maybe, but not me. I'm not…'

The furrow of uncertainty in Emma's brow cut through his libidinous thoughts.

'Not what?'

Emma looked away and he sensed she was going to prevaricate. Then, instead, she shrugged and met his eye. 'I'm not a model or a sophisticate. I'm not…' Again that telling pause. 'Gorgeous and glamorous.'

Christo heard the hitch of her breath and realised that despite her defiant stare, as if daring him to judge her, Emma really couldn't see her own attractiveness.

But then, he hadn't in the beginning. Originally he'd thought her pretty and charming, but not in a league with the beauties he knew. Somewhere along the line, though, Christo had come to appreciate his wife's character and fire, her unique beauty.

'Who'd want a model?' he murmured, stroking a fingertip down her cheek. 'Most of them are scrawny and too afraid to enjoy a proper meal.' He paused, holding her eyes. 'You're beautiful, Emma. I defy any woman tonight to outshine you.'

Her eyes widened and a flush rose up her throat and into her cheeks. She swung away. 'Don't lie, Christo.' Her voice sounded muffled, twisting something in his belly. 'I've had enough lies from you to last a lifetime.'

Stymied, Christo stared at her profile, proud and, he realised, hurt. He was damned if he told the truth about her beauty and damned if he didn't. He should drop the subject, yet he was reluctant to leave it.

Emma hadn't struck him as a woman with hang-ups about her looks. Then memory pierced him. She'd admitted some time ago that she'd heard his conversation with Damen about why he'd married her. He recalled saying she wasn't his type. That her cousin was more his style, sexy and flamboyant.

Christo dragged in a slow breath, battling self-loathing. He plucked the necklace from the case and stepped behind his wife. Carefully he draped it around her neck, feeling her shiver as his hands brushed her nape. His own hands were unsteady. From the thwarted lust that had stalked him for weeks, or something else?

The clasp closed, he palmed her bare shoulders, fingers splaying across warm, satiny skin, and turned her to face the mirror.

'Look.'

Her chin jerked up, her narrowed eyes meeting his in the mirror.

'Not at me.' He let his gaze drift over the woman before him. 'You're stunning, Emma.' And it wasn't just because of the magnificent tourmaline and diamond collar around her slender throat. It was because of the woman who stood before him, trembling but as stiff as a soldier on parade.

Emma's eyes locked on the reflection of the man behind her as she battled not to lean back against all that delicious heat.

Christo Karides had treated her appallingly. He'd used her for his own advantage. Yet sometimes, like tonight, she fought to remember he was the enemy. He seemed too much like the caring lover she'd once believed him to be.

Take the expression in his eyes. Despite his stern tone, his eyes caressed her, made her feel warm and fuzzy inside. It wasn't the glaze of sexual possessiveness she'd seen in the past but something more tender.

Her thoughts terrified her. Hadn't she learned her lesson, reading emotions and motivations into Christo's actions that just weren't there?

She made to pull away but his hands stopped her. Not because his grip was hard, but because at that very moment those long fingers swept wide over the bare curve of her shoulders, massaging gently.

'Look, Emma.' His voice was soft.

Oh, she was looking. Her gaze swept from those broad shoulders to that solid jaw, past the tiny nick of a scar to his mobile mouth. Then up that decisive nose to eyes that glowed the colour of the sky at dusk.

Emma dragged in an abrupt breath and found herself inhaling that heady signature of cedar, leather and spice with that underlying note of male skin.

The scent shot to her brain, and her womb, and suddenly Emma wasn't looking just at Christo but at the pair of them. He with his hands on her body, she canting back towards him as if drawn to a magnet.

Suddenly she saw herself as others would. Wearing couture clothes and fabulous gems because Christo Karides demanded the best. A swift glance confirmed what she'd seen before. The makeover turned her into someone else. Someone glossy enough to match a billionaire, if only for an evening.

Heart hammering, Emma broke away. Tonight she'd play the doting bride and counter any negative press stories. But she'd be herself, not some puppet on a string dancing to Christo's tune. If he didn't like that, then that was entirely his problem.

CHAPTER NINE

CHRISTO COUNTED THE final items to be auctioned as the charity event drew to a close. Only half a dozen more.

He set his jaw and concentrated on keeping his touch light as he drew his fingertips across the soft skin of Emma's shoulder. She leaned close, her tantalising honey scent teasing his nostrils. The press of her hip on the seat next to his and the rounded contour of her breast against his side stirred a libido already at breaking point.

Telling himself she only did it to play the besotted bride didn't help. His body didn't care about her motivations, just the imprint of her warm curves and how much closer they could get once they left here.

No one bid on the next item. Christo frowned at the delay as Emma turned from speaking to the entrepreneur sitting on her other side and eased back into his embrace.

Fire stormed through his body, drenching him in heat.

Still no bids. Christo raised his hand, nodding to the auctioneer, who beamed back. It was past time they moved on to the final items and ended this. The event had dragged intolerably.

It had begun well enough. Emma had played her part admirably, sticking by his side and not flinching when he pulled her close. The fact she trembled when he did, Christo read as a positive sign. Emma had always been responsive to him and that hadn't changed. Did she know her body's reaction gave her away every time?

She'd been an enormous hit with his acquaintances. Far from being a shy mouse, she'd been quietly assured, conversing easily with everyone. She had the knack of drawing people out, truly listening to what they had to say and keeping the conversation rolling, even when it wasn't about her. She'd been everything he could have hoped for and more. As well as being articulate and sociable, she was...nice.

It seemed such a paltry word. But to Christo, having grown up in a world where appearances were everything, where trust was rare and self-interest dominated, Emma's sweet honesty and generous spirit felt precious.

He wasn't the only one to think so. All night he'd been congratulated and envied. In fact, he'd noted a few guys considering her a little too warmly. Till Christo had warned them off with a speaking stare.

Now he was heartily sick of the crowd. Of being congratulated on his lovely bride when that bride still kept her guard up against him. When this nearness was for show and she'd re-erect the barriers between them as soon as they were alone.

He wanted more. Much more.

He wanted his wife. Frustration grew with every minute and every brush of his hand against silky bare skin.

'You're bidding? I didn't think you'd be interested in this item.' Emma sounded surprised and he shrugged, willing the auctioneer to hurry.

'It's an important cause and no one else was bidding.'

Finally someone else did. The auctioneer caught Christo's eye and he read a mix of doubt and expectancy that indicated the man would drag this out in the hope of securing a much bigger profit. So much for Christo's scheme to end this quickly.

Supressing a sigh, he raised his hand and made a bid calculated to win. Whispers rippled around the room.

The auctioneer looked stunned, but recovered quickly to ask for more bids. There were none. Christo's price was too high for anyone else.

With a slam of the gavel, bidding closed.

Five more items to go. Christo stretched his legs and

tried to stifle his impatience. Emma moved, her body twisting against his, and the molten heat through his lower body turned to forged steel. His skin felt too tight and his lungs cramped.

'What are you going to do with it?'

'Sorry?' He turned to meet her eyes and felt the pause in her breathing as their gazes meshed.

Oh, yes. This desire was definitely mutual. She couldn't conceal the minute, give-away proof of her body's reaction to his.

All the more reason to get out of here as soon as possible and persuade her to put an end to this intolerable sexual frustration.

'The prize. Are you going to use it?'

Despite the confusion in Emma's expression, Christo read the glaze of heat in her eyes. Anticipation slammed into him. Tonight the waiting would end.

Strange to think that originally he'd viewed her as passably pretty. Merely a convenient spouse. She was anything but convenient and far, far beyond merely passable. Had he ever wanted a woman like this?

'Christo?'

'I'm not sure.'

Suspicion dawned in her fine eyes. The corner of her mouth curved into the tiniest hint of amusement. Christo's gaze locked on those glossy lips that had driven him to distraction all night.

Emma leaned close, her words whispering heat across his face as she murmured, 'You do *know* what you bought, don't you?'

He shrugged. 'I was more interested in helping them get through the programme quickly.'

Her breath hitched, her eyes widened and then she was laughing. The sound brought an answering smile to his mouth and an intense feeling of wellbeing. But at the same time that husky chuckle curled around his belly like a lasso, drawing tense nerves even tighter.

Beyond Emma heads turned. People leaned forward to hear the joke but she was totally focused on him. Just the way he liked her.

'That's very noble of you.' Still she smiled. No shadows in her expression now, just mirth and approval.

Christo was surprised at how good it felt when Emma looked at him that way. With shared understanding and humour.

'Don't you want to know what you spent all that money on?'

He shrugged. 'A car?' There'd been a sports car coming up for auction. When she shook her head he tried again. 'A boat?' Not that he needed another cruiser.

Emma shook her head, amusement and approval continuing to dance in her eyes. It struck him he could get used to her approval. It made him feel good.

'So, enlighten me, Emma.' His voice slowed on her name, savouring it. Or, more correctly, savouring the flicker of awareness in those bright eyes that shone tonight more green than brown.

She tilted her head down, whether to keep their conversation private or to avoid his eyes, he couldn't tell. 'An all-expenses-paid trip for a family of four to France, including a couple of days at Euro Disney.' Abruptly she looked up, her eyebrows rising. 'Are you excited to go on all the rides?'

His laughter shouldn't affect her like this. As if he'd turned her insides to melted caramel and added a huge dollop of sexual desire.

People laughed all the time. But Christo's deep, uninhibited chuckle affected her in the strangest way.

Not so strange. You've lusted after him all night.
All night? Far longer!

Just because he could afford to donate a small fortune to a children's charity didn't make him a decent man. Just as his smile didn't make him any less dangerous.

But it was hard to keep him in a box marked 'ogre' or 'blackmailer' when she saw him like this. Or head down with Anthea, working together on a crayon drawing.

Emma released a silent sigh and felt another layer of her defences slip away.

Face it. You've enjoyed being with him tonight. You like snuggling up against him, feeling his arm around you.

You like the admiration in his eyes.

Even if the admiration was for a glossy façade that wasn't the real Emma. Underneath the couture gown and priceless gems she was the same as always—ordinary. No makeover could change that.

'Hey.' A warm finger curled under her chin, tilting her face up. 'What's wrong?'

For the briefest moment, Emma contemplated telling her husband the truth. That she still cared for him despite her attempts not to. That part of her wanted him to care for *her*, not because she brushed up well enough to attend a gala social event but because he found her interesting, because he liked her for who she really was.

'Nothing.' She paused and summoned a smile, pulling back a little till his hand fell away. 'What are you going to do about the prize?'

For a long moment Christo studied her, as if probing to discover what went on inside her head.

'Give it to Giorgos.'

'Giorgos?'

'Our building's concierge. I introduced you to him today. His wife lost her job two weeks ago and their youngest is just out of hospital. They could do with a treat.'

Emma nodded as Christo turned to the event organiser who'd come up to talk with him.

Every time she reminded herself Christo wasn't worth pining over, he surprised her. Such as now, with his plan to give the holiday to his concierge. How many people who lived in the luxury apartment building even knew the man's name? Christo knew it and far more. He was genuinely interested in people. It wasn't the attitude of a man who viewed others as pawns.

Then there was his willingness to give Anthea's nanny a second chance. His patience with his little niece, despite his initial reserve. Plus there'd been his surprise gift for Dora, a bright-red motor scooter she now used whenever she needed to travel the several kilometres between the villa and the nearest town.

Emma had been stunned by his thoughtfulness. And by her lack of perception. Dora had mentioned she didn't like driving Papou's big car that sat gleaming in the garage. But Emma had forgotten the local bus only went by twice a day. Nor had she noticed the older woman was often fatigued or that she often made the trip on foot. Being distracted by her own problems was no excuse. Nor was the fact she'd grown up thinking Dora indomitable. That she'd come to rely on the housekeeper too much. It was Christo who'd arranged extra staff to assist Dora now the villa was occupied.

It was discomfiting, discovering her husband was more perceptive and generous than she'd credited. That he'd taken it upon himself to help out with something she should have dealt with.

The trouble was, Christo wasn't just a ruthless tycoon. There were times when he was plain likeable. That made him hard to resist. Especially when tonight all her not so dormant longings reawakened.

His arm tightened around her shoulders and he leaned in, breath tickling her ear and sending shivers of erotic awareness rippling through her.

'Ready to go?'

'But the auction?' She swung around towards the stage, belatedly registering the wave of applause that signalled the end of the event.

'We can skip the final speeches. I want to be alone with you.' Christo's eyes locked onto hers and the sizzle in her blood became a burst of fire.

Emma opened her mouth to protest. But what was the point? She'd tried and tried but resisting had become impossible.

Maybe it was time to reach out and take what she wanted. She was a woman with a woman's needs. Surely she could satisfy this physical craving and reduce the stress of trying to resist the irresistible?

She couldn't love Christo after what he'd done but she wanted him. She had nothing to lose by sleeping with him.

In fact, that contract he'd signed made it a condition of her escaping his influence. Though right now she had no thoughts of escape.

Nervous, she licked her lips. Instantly his attention dropped to the movement. Emma heard his breath catch.

Suddenly it was so easy. Because for the first time they were equals.

'I'd like that.'

The words were barely out of her mouth when he scooped her up to stand against him. Their farewells were rushed and she saw knowing glances as she grabbed her bag and wrap and said goodnight.

She'd liked the people at their table and enjoyed their conversation, but she was as eager as Christo to leave. So eager that she didn't protest as he guided her through the crowd with one arm still round her, his broad palm on her hip. Heat splayed from the spot, up her side, round to her breasts and straight down to her achy, hollow core.

Emma didn't even mind when photographers pressed close as they left the building and got into a waiting car.

All her attention was on Christo and the charge of erotic energy sparking between them.

Finally they were alone, a privacy screen cutting them off from the driver.

'At last.' The words were a groan, as if from a man exhausted. But Christo didn't look worn out. He looked taut, thrumming with energy.

When he reached out his hand, palm up, she put her fingers in his and felt that pulse of power race through her. It was like thunder rolling in from a massive storm front, a deep vibration heavy with building promise.

Emma couldn't prevent a shiver of reaction. She'd never experienced the like.

Christo nodded as his fingers clamped round her hand, as if he too felt that overwhelming inevitability. His smile of understanding looked strained.

That strain on his severely sculpted features flattened any final hesitation. This wasn't Christo seducing her. This was the pair of them caught in something elemental and all-consuming.

'Come here.' His voice was a rough whisper that did crazy things to her insides. Yet, despite the peremptory command, even now Christo didn't haul her close or try to force her. This was Emma's choice, as he'd promised.

She slid across the seat till she came up against the steamy heat of his big frame. One long arm wrapped around her, turning her towards him. She needed no urging. Her palm slipped under his jacket, moulding the rigid swell of his chest muscles through his fine shirt. Emma shivered at how good that felt. How much more she wanted to feel.

For a second those thundercloud eyes held hers, then Christo lowered his head and took her mouth.

Despite the urgency thrumming through them, his kiss was restrained, as if he fought to control the elemental storm that threatened to sweep them away.

He tasted of black coffee and something indefinable that set Emma's senses ablaze. Her hands clutched and she leaned in, needing more, far more than this gentle caress. Inside she was a threshing mass of need.

'Kiss me properly,' she hissed against his lips. She'd craved this so long. All that time he'd been carefully courting her she'd yearned for the taste of his unbridled passion. 'Please.'

Christo pulled back just enough to look deep into her eyes. Then, as if reading the hunger she could barely express, he planted his hands at her waist and hoisted her up to sit sideways across his lap. Emma had a bare moment to register his formidable strength, to lift her so easily in such a confined space. Then he kissed her again and nothing else existed but Christo and the magic he wrought.

There was fire. Emma felt it lick her insides, flaring brighter by the second. Frenzy. Rough demand and eager response. Tongues sliding together and mouths fused. Hearts thundering in tune. The roar of blood in her ears and bliss in her soul. Steely arms binding her to him.

This was the kiss she'd dreamed about in her virginal bed. No wonder she'd been frustrated and jittery all this time, unable to settle to anything useful after nights with too little rest and too many hours imagining Christo making love to her.

He tasted glorious. He felt even better. But there was more. Passion far beyond her experience, beckoning her deeper, simultaneously satisfying her desire and increasing it.

Emma's ribs tightened around her lungs as she forgot to breathe. But she couldn't have stopped if her life had depended on it. She clutched him as if she could meld their bodies through sheer force of will. She twisted closer, stymied by her fitted dress. There was something she needed even more than his lips on hers and those satisfyingly hard arms pinioning her close.

Emma shifted on Christo's lap, trying to ease that compelling restlessness.

Then without warning he tilted her back so she was no longer upright but supported only by his arm. Foggily she wondered why this felt so insanely perfect when at any other time she'd chafe at a show of superiority by her husband.

Her husband.

The word snapped her brain into a belated stir of worry, till Christo's hand on her bare knee obliterated extraneous thoughts.

Instantly that restless, needy feeling between her legs intensified. Her breath stalled as Christo plunged his tongue into her mouth in a lascivious swirl that made her nipples ache and tighten. At the same time his big, warm hand stroked up her thigh, rucking the silk dress higher and higher till air wafted...

A sudden hubbub erupted. Christo jolted upright, taking her with him as he ripped his hand free of her dress. She heard strange voices, questions and, like a dark undercurrent to the unfamiliar noise, the sound of Christo cursing quietly but ferociously.

For a second nothing made sense. Then out of the darkness a light flashed and then another.

Emma realised the back door of the limo was open. An attendant stood holding it wide. Behind him a huddle of people surged close, cameras snapping.

Paparazzi. Taking photos of her lying sprawled across Christo, his tongue down her throat and his hand up her dress.

In that instant glorious elation turned to wordless embarrassment. She shrivelled and couldn't quite get her body to move, to cover herself.

But Christo was already doing that. Not covering her, since there was nothing at hand to drape over her, but leaning forward, putting himself between her and those avid faces.

He said something she didn't hear and moments later the door slammed.

As if that movement released her from her shocked stasis, Emma suddenly found the strength to slither off his lap and onto the seat, scrambling to put some distance between them.

Eyes wide, she stared up at Christo. They were parked outside a brightly lit building and there was enough light to see his face. Far from being distressed or self-conscious at finding himself photographed in the act of making love in the back seat, he looked as solid and calm as ever.

As if making love to her *had* been an *act*?

Pain stabbed her heaving chest, transfixing her. Desperately she searched for some sign of annoyance or embarrassment on those proud features. She found none.

Had he *expected* the intrusion on their privacy?

Could he really be so calculating?

Everything inside Emma froze. She'd have sworn the moisture in her mouth turned to icicles as the idea hit.

Christo was breathing heavily, but that was understandable, given how their mouths had just been fused together. His hair was rumpled where she'd tunnelled her fingers along his scalp. His bow tie was undone and his shirt askew. But he looked unfazed by the furore outside the car. Unfazed and insanely hot.

Eyes on her, he pressed a button and gave instructions to the driver. His voice was crisp. Emma knew if she tried to talk right now it would emerge as a breathless squawk.

He watched her closely, as if trying to read her reaction. Was he wondering if she realised this had been a set up? Just like their wedding?

Had he really used her so callously? But then, given his track record…

The last shreds of heat inside Emma disintegrated, leaving her chilled to the marrow.

Even her fury, emerging from that white-hot sear of mortification, was cold. It whipped through her like the icy winter wind that swept Melbourne from the Antarctic.

'I apologise, Emma. The driver's original instructions were to take us to a restaurant where the press would be waiting to take photos.' Christo lifted his wide shoulders a scant centimetre. 'I was distracted when we left the auction and forgot to tell him to take us straight home instead. It was my mistake.'

'How very convenient.'

'Pardon?'

Emma lifted her hand to her hair, hauling up the soft waves he'd dislodged as he'd kissed her and jabbing in pins so hard Christo almost winced, imagining the grazes on her scalp. He wanted to reach out and grab her wrists, tell her the haphazard attempts to rectify the sophisticated hairstyle weren't working, and that besides he preferred it down. But she was upset enough. She wouldn't thank him.

The horror on her face smote his conscience. He shouldn't have let it happen. Should have protected her better. Even a woman who'd grown up in the public eye would cringe at the sort of pictures he knew would cover the tabloids in the morning.

Emma had looked wanton, beautiful and thoroughly aroused and the thought of anyone but him seeing her that way was like a knife to his gut. She was *his* and his alone.

'How incredibly convenient that you should *forget* to change the instructions. And that the doorman from the restaurant should open the car without a signal we were ready.'

Christo registered the acid in her tone and frowned. 'That's what doormen do. They open doors.'

He tamped down annoyance at her implication. She'd had a shock.

Emma's mouth turned mulish and her chin reared high in an attitude he knew too well. Stubborn defiance. 'And I suppose you had no idea we were outside the restaurant, even though you know Athens so well?' Her voice dripped shards of sarcasm that grazed his already smarting conscience.

'Let me get this straight. You're accusing me of luring you into a compromising situation just to embarrass you publicly?' Christo picked the words out slowly, barely crediting her implication.

'Of course not.' The vein of righteous indignation pulsing through him slowed. He'd been mistaken to think Emma could believe... 'Not to embarrass me specifically. I'm sure that was just collateral damage as far as you're concerned.' She dropped her hands to her lap and belatedly snicked her seatbelt closed as if to reinforce the distance between them. 'You did it to prove we're hot for each other, didn't you? That all's well between the bride and groom and any rumours that I'd left you were laughable.'

Her voice wobbled on the last word, but Christo couldn't feel sympathy.

Her accusation impugned his integrity. What sort of man did she think he was? So desperate he'd let the world into such a private moment?

A ripple of distaste coursed through him, starting from the bitterness filling his mouth and ending down at the soles of his feet.

He'd been vilified and taunted by his father whenever the old man thought he wasn't callous or committed enough to shoulder the mantle of the Karides corporation. He'd grown accustomed to press reports that misinterpreted or even invented facts about him. He accepted as inevitable that there were probably only a handful of people in the world, like his PA and his old friend Damen, who really knew him. But that didn't mean he'd shrug off such a deliberate insult.

An insult from the woman who, fifteen minutes ago, had all but begged him to take her in the back of this car.

A woman who'd driven him crazy these last weeks with lust and frustration.

A woman whose actions in running from him after their wedding had left him using all his influence and ingenuity to avoid a scandal that would damage them both.

The limo glided down into the underground car park of his apartment building. The increased lighting showed Christo a woman who was not only defiant but sneering.

Something cracked inside him.

'We'll continue this in the apartment.' He opened his door and got out, leaving the driver to get Emma's door.

The trip to the penthouse was completed in thick silence. The sort that wrapped around the lungs and squeezed mercilessly.

What was it about this woman that made him feel so furious, so resentful, so blindsided?

So *gutted*. As if, despite being in the right, he could have done better?

Christo had spent a lifetime learning to be top of his game, top of *any* game he played. He'd survived thirty-one years riding the rough with the smooth, learning never to expect too much. But nothing had prepared him for Emma.

Christo held the front door open to let her sweep past, nose in the air, green jewels swinging from her ears with each step. She crossed the foyer and entered the sitting room with an undulating sashay of her hips in that tight dress that might have been due to her high heels but which instinct told him was a deliberate provocation.

Did she know she played with fire?

In the car she'd driven him to the brink of insanity with her untrammelled eagerness. His wife kissed like an angel, but a woefully inexperienced one. He'd bet his last dollar Emma hadn't thought through the effect of such blatant sexual challenge. If she had, she'd probably run and lock herself in her bedroom.

The separate bedroom he'd arranged because he'd foolishly agreed to let her make the first move.

Christo gritted his teeth but made himself close the door quietly before following her.

She swung around, face flushed, eyes febrile and hair a delectable mess that made her look as though she'd just got out of bed.

His belly clenched painfully, re-igniting frustration. Even now his wife couldn't conceal the fact she wanted him. She devoured him with her eyes, her tongue darting out to slick her lips. Her breasts rose so high with each breath they strained the strapless bodice and her hard nipples signalled arousal. Anger, yes, but desire too.

It struck him that her indignation was a convenient shield for other emotions.

Christo shoved his hands in his pockets, rocking back on his heels. 'I've had enough, Emma.'

'*You've* had enough? I—'

'It's my turn to talk.' His tone was even but held the note of authority he'd honed over years as a CEO.

She took another hefty breath that made him wonder if her breasts might pop free of the green silk, then nodded.

'Maybe I should have been more upfront with you.'

Emma's eyes rounded, as if stunned at his admission.

'Maybe I should have spelled out exactly why I wanted to marry you.'

Not that it would have changed anything. He'd been determined to find the right woman and Emma was definitely it, despite her annoying habit of throwing up obstacles and questioning his motives.

'Maybe I shouldn't have assumed you knew there was

a business element to the arrangement. I shouldn't have assumed, wrongly, that your grandfather had discussed that with you.' He paused. 'I could have told you myself about Anthea.'

Except he'd been worried news of a ready-made family might deter Emma and he'd been utterly focused on putting his ring on her finger.

'But since then I've been completely upfront. From the moment I found you in Corfu I've been utterly honest with you.' Christo felt a bubble of mirthless humour rise. 'So honest, it shocked you.' The look of horror on her face when he'd mentioned sharing a bed had been both a blow to his ego and a spur to his determination.

Emma opened her mouth to speak but he shook his head. 'I told you we were going to the auction then to an exclusive restaurant so we could be seen together.' Christo drew a slow breath, still finding it hard to believe he'd so lost control that he'd been unprepared when the limo door had opened.

He never lost control. Never.

'I also apologised and explained how it happened. I forgot to tell the driver to bring us here because I was concentrating on you. Specifically, how I was going to strip you bare and make love to every centimetre of that delectable body.'

Emma's shocked hiss was loud in the quiet room, reminding him that she was a sexual innocent. That didn't excuse her accusations. Except that it was convenient for her to distort the truth.

Christo stalked closer. She couldn't hide the shimmer of nervous excitement in her eyes. But he wasn't in the mood to play to her tune any more.

'Tonight was an honest mistake. I have no more interest than you in having compromising pictures of us spread across the news. I prefer to keep my love life private.'

Not that he *had* a love life now. Because he'd given his word not to push her. This woman drove him mad!

'Don't imagine conspiracies where there are none. I don't operate like that, as you'd know if you'd paid attention lately.' Christo drew in a calming breath, but to little effect. He was past the point of no return.

'What's between us is real, Emma, and I'm not talking about a marriage certificate. I'm talking about desire, lust, attraction—whatever you want to call it. You can't run from it, though that seems to be your style. Instead of facing me after the wedding, you ran off like a hurt child.'

Her mouth dropped open at the jibe but he kept going, driven by the need to slash through all the pretence.

Christo closed the space between them, feeling the inevitable shimmer of awareness as he stepped up against her. It intensified to a riotous clamour as he touched his fingertip to her chin and tilted it up.

Bewildered eyes met his and he might have felt sorry for her if her games weren't driving him to the edge. It took every scintilla of control not to haul her close and kiss her into mindless abandon. No doubt then she'd claim he'd forced her. That she hadn't really wanted him.

'It's time you faced what's between us instead of pretending it doesn't exist or inventing excuses not to trust me.' Christo's voice ground low as his patience frayed. 'I've been patient. I've given you my name and my word. I want to give you my body too. But I won't be the butt of your lame excuses or manufactured obstacles because you're too scared to take what we both know you want.'

He stepped away, ignoring the confusion in her face.

'When you grow up, when you're ready to follow through, let me know.' Christo turned on his heel and strode away.

CHAPTER TEN

EMMA WRENCHED OFF the taps and grabbed an oversized towel. The shower had done nothing to relieve her distress. Warm water usually relaxed her. But tonight the fine spray had needled her skin like Christo's words needled her conscience.

She hadn't run away like a child!

Had she?

But why should she have stayed? He'd behaved monstrously, making her believe he loved her.

Except most of that had been wishful thinking. He'd been considerate and kind to her, so she'd *wanted* him to love her because she'd fallen for him.

As for making excuses or throwing up obstacles...

Emma briskly rubbed the towel over her body. But instead of expensive plush fabric, it felt like sandpaper. Like the graze of Christo's accusations.

Firming her mouth, she stepped out and dragged off her shower cap. Her hair fell around her shoulders but, instead of its familiar weight, she imagined his touch, so strong yet so tender, as he held her to him and kissed her.

Breathing heavily, she slung the towel over a rail and turned to get her nightwear. Except she'd been so furious and distressed, she'd stomped into the bathroom without grabbing anything to wear.

As she turned the beautiful green dress, discarded over a chair, caught her eye. Then the exquisite jewellery on the marble bathroom counter, sparkling under the light so much she could almost imagine it winked mockingly. As if reminding her that tonight's outfit wasn't her style. She was no glamorous sophisticate. She and Christo didn't fit.

Or was she doing it again? Making excuses and manufacturing obstacles?

Emma's mouth crumpled and her heart dived towards the honey-toned marble floor as suspicion solidified into something like certainty.

Christo had done the wrong thing, no doubt about that.

But shouldn't she at least have faced him and called him on that straight away? Shouldn't she have had more gumption than to run and hide like a child?

Misery curdled her belly. Her disappointment had been so acute, her heartbreak so painful, she'd needed to escape. But there was no escaping the complicated truth between them now.

Christo was right. Remarkably, she wanted him every bit as much as he seemed to want her, physically at any rate.

Desire fizzed in her blood whenever she saw him, or thought about him. But instead of doing something about it she'd looked for distractions to avoid facing it. Taking umbrage when she'd thought he'd brought a lover to the villa, though if she'd thought about it for even a second she'd have known Christo had more class than that. Accusing him of engineering that scene for the press tonight when that was laughable. Especially as she had perfect recall of his erection, steely hard against her hip.

Christo hadn't pretended to desire her. And she knew how vigorously he protected his privacy. One of his first actions after having found her in Corfu was to arrange perimeter security to stop intruders and prying press.

He'd wanted her. Plus he'd made her feel wonderful tonight in so many ways. His interest in what she had to say. The pride in his voice as he'd introduced her, and the way he'd kept steering conversations away from people she didn't know and into general areas so she could contribute. The warmth in his eyes as they'd shared amusement at some of tonight's auction items.

His possessiveness when men had got too close.

Emma shivered despite the warmth of the steamy bathroom and realised she was still naked.

Her gaze caught her reflection in the mirror that took up one wall. She was still the same old Emma. Not stupendous in any way. An average body and an ordinary face. Nice legs, she'd been told, but she'd always wished they were longer. As she'd wished for wheat-blonde hair and an elegant nose instead of one too close to being snub.

The only real difference she saw, apart from hair a shade lighter from the Greek sun, was the way her eyes glowed. Had they been so bright before?

It didn't matter. What mattered was why they glowed.

Christo. He had a talent for getting under her skin and making her feel more for him than she should. Once it had been love. She hurried to assure herself she was cured of that. What she felt was simple animal attraction.

Inevitably her mind turned to the salacious, outrageous demand he'd made that first day on Corfu. That she spend at least one night in his bed to claim her inheritance.

No matter how she'd told herself he couldn't force her, she'd never been able to forget it completely. She wanted to be with him and that need to discover how it would be grew daily. As if the seed, once planted in her mind, had grown till it obliterated all else. Now was her chance to satisfying her craving and her curiosity. Then afterwards, if she wanted to, she could walk away.

She shook her head. This wasn't about her inheritance or Christo's outlandish proposition. It was about satisfying her needs.

What would she do? Run and hide, as he expected? Play safe and try to avoid him?

Or throw herself into the fire and hope she survived?

Emma knew a moment's terrible self-doubt as inclination fought a determination to stand up for herself, not with words this time, but action.

Then she grabbed a plush robe from a hook and shrugged it on, cinching it around her waist.

The rap of her knuckles on the door of the master suite sounded over-loud. Emma waited, heart pounding, head tilted forward to listen. Nothing. Was Christo asleep?

Surely not. They'd only parted twenty minutes ago.

Firming her lips, she turned the doorknob and entered. Predictably the master suite was vast and luxurious. What surprised her was how comfortable it felt. She had an impression of parchment walls and splashes of rich teal that reminded her of the deep sea off Corfu on a sunny day. There was a book-lined wall and a leather lounge.

But what drew her eye was the filmy curtain riffling in the breeze at the open door, and beyond it the tall shadow on the terrace.

'Christo?' With numb fingers she shut the door behind her. That was all the time it took for him to step inside.

He still wore dress trousers but his tie was gone and his feet bare. Rolled sleeves revealed strong forearms that looked so good, her insides gave a needy leap. His formal white shirt gaped to reveal a slice of dark olive skin dusted with black hair that made her mouth dry.

Emma had seen him almost naked in his swim shorts, but somehow that V of tantalising flesh seemed just as decadently tempting. She gulped and lifted her gaze, noting the way his hair stood up, as if he'd clutched it. And the glitter of dark, assessing eyes.

'What is it, Emma?'

'I came to apologise.' She sucked in a quick breath. 'I was wrong to accuse you the way I did. I'm sorry.'

He pushed his hands into his trouser pockets, drawing her attention to his powerful thighs.

'Apology accepted. Thank you.'

Still he stood, simply watching.

She couldn't work out if that was anger emanating from him or something else. A voice in her head told her it was time to leave before she made a fool of herself or did something irreversibly dangerous.

Instead she stood her ground. Adrenalin shot through her blood in a classic 'fight or flight' response to this big, bold, provoking man who watched her as if he had all the time in the world.

'I didn't think before I spoke,' she offered.

He inclined his head, as if that was obvious.

Emma shifted her weight from one foot to another. He wasn't going to make this easy for her, was he?

Finally he spoke. 'It's late. Was there anything else?' His tone wasn't encouraging. He made no move towards her and Emma knew a craven urge to whip round and escape to the guest room.

But she was stronger than that.

Or perhaps just needier.

'Yes.' The word emerged too loud. 'I came because I want you to make lo—' She stopped. That wasn't what either of them wanted to hear. 'I want to have sex with you.'

Emma didn't know what she'd expected but it was more than she got. Christo didn't seem to move a muscle. Did he even blink?

What was he waiting for?

Then it struck her. She'd already said yes to him once tonight, only to turn on him after that mistake at the restaurant.

Maybe words weren't enough.

Or—the devastating thought sliced through her—maybe he'd changed his mind.

'If you still want me?' Ignoring the slight unevenness in her voice, she lifted her chin.

'I do.' The two words in that slow, deep voice sounded like a vow. Her nape prickled as she recalled their wedding vows. Then she shoved the recollection aside. This was different. She felt that here, now, there was only honesty between them.

Gathering her nerve, Emma paced forward, not stopping till they stood toe to toe.

The heady scent of virile male tantalised her nostrils and the breeze through the open door stirred her hair. What she read in those smoky eyes made heat flare across her skin. The dazzle of hunger was so potent, so raw, it dried her mouth and made her tremble.

Christo read Emma's nerves in her wide eyes and the racing pulse at her neck. She swallowed and he wanted to lick his way down her throat. He'd hungered for her for so long. He'd made allowances for her inexperience and hurt. He'd denied himself because he'd understood she needed time. Tonight his patience had reached its limit.

Which was why he wouldn't make a move till he knew she was absolutely committed. That she wouldn't change her mind again.

Swathed in an oversized bathrobe, Emma looked vulnerable, yet sexy and determined. It was a contradiction he didn't understand but he was fast losing the capacity for thought as she stared up with that provocative pout and her body clearly naked beneath the towelling.

He was torn between protectiveness and rampant lust.

'Show me.' His voice was a harsh whisper through lips that barely moved. His whole body ached from being held in check. From fighting the need to take.

He blinked when she stepped closer. He felt her warmth against him, her breath a puff of heat against his chest as she reached for his shirt and began to undo it.

Christo sucked in a desperate breath as her knuckles brushed his skin in a delicate, moving pattern designed to unstring his tendons and loosen his resolve. She leaned in and the honey scent of her hair infiltrated his brain, sending it into overload.

Abdominal muscles spasmed at she reached his trousers and paused.

Glowing eyes met his. Questioning eyes.

'Are you sure?' It cost him to speak. 'If we start this there'll be no turning back.'

She dropped her hands and stepped away. Disappointment smote him, so severe, he tasted it like poison on his tongue.

Christo was silently cursing his restraint when Emma tugged the belt of her robe. With a defiant tilt of her head, and a sensuous little shimmy that undid him, she let the material drop.

Naked, she was perfection.

Christo's heart beat so fast, it tripped and stole his breath.

Pale skin, pink nipples, and a V of darker hair nestling between her slender thighs, accentuating the impossibly sweet curve from waist to hips.

He'd wanted her when she was a convenient bride, acquired for purely practical reasons.

He'd been hot for her as she'd confronted him wearing only attitude and a blue bikini.

These last three weeks he'd ached for her at an even deeper level, haunted by her laugh, her sweetness with Anthea and Dora and, tonight, with him. Even when she defied him and drove him crazy, it only raised the scale of his wanting.

'Christo?'

He dragged his gaze up and saw her bottom lip caught between her teeth. Hesitation in her eyes.

Emma was about to turn away when his eyes met hers and blue fire welded her soles to the floor. Heat drenched her and suddenly doubt fled.

Big hands took hers and hooked them into the front of his trousers above the zip.

'Don't stop now,' he drawled as he dragged that snowy shirt up from his trousers and shrugged it off, leaving her in possession of a view that dried her mouth.

For ages she stared at the shift and play of bare, taut flesh over muscle. Then her brain kicked into gear and onto the task of undoing his trousers. It was tricky, possibly because her hands shook.

Finally, with a sigh that swelled her chest, she got them undone, but not before her knuckles brushed the tantalising length of his erection. She shivered, trying to imagine herself accommodating all that hardness. But the shiver wasn't all anxiety. Mostly it was excitement.

His trousers fell to the floor and still Christo stood, unmoving. Swallowing, Emma crooked her fingers into the top of his boxers and slid them down. The place between her legs throbbed with heat as she watched the reveal of yet more golden skin. Then his shaft sprang free and she jumped, staring.

As if reading her moment of panic, Christo lifted his hand to her cheek in a butterfly caress that eased her riot of nerves. But the riot started again as his finger trawled down, over her chin and collarbone to her breast, where delicately he circled her nipple. Emma shifted, trying to assuage the edgy sensation inside when his other hand captured hers and brought it against him.

'There's nothing here to be afraid of.' His voice wound around her as his eyes held hers.

Instinctively her fingers curled round his length, slowly exploring the fascinating velvet over steel combination. At the movement, Christo's eyes flickered, the corners of his mouth pulling down as if with tension. Gripping a little tighter, she slid her hand again and watched that tell-tale drag of his lips.

The realisation that she did that to him boosted Emma's confidence.

'I'm not afraid.'

But her smile ended in a gasp as his other hand flirted across her thighs, then slipped between her legs, right up against folds that felt swollen and wet. Gently he slid his fingers down, arrowing to the exact spot where sensation centred. He pressed, and she jolted as a current of electricity snapped through her.

Emma swayed forward, needing more, almost sighing with relief when his hand at her breast opened to mould her more firmly. In answer her fingers tightened around Christo till he murmured, 'Easy,' and she loosened her hold. Needing more, she planted her left hand on his chest, solid with muscle and tickly with that smattering of dark hair.

His heart beat steadily beneath her touch, the rhythm reassuring as she found herself in completely new territory.

The big hand between her legs moved again, sending sparks showering through her, then dipping even further till one finger slid home and Emma gasped at the shocking unfamiliarity of it. But shock turned to eagerness as he withdrew, then slid home again, evoking wonderful sensations. She found her pelvis rocking with the movement.

Another slide and the friction made her breath stop. Stunned, she stared into Christo's eyes and couldn't look away. Surely they should be in bed, lying down before…?

'We can't.' Her words faded as his thumb pressed that sensitive nub and she trembled all over.

'Believe me, sweetheart, we can. We can do whatever you like.' His words would have reassured Emma, except she read excitement in his dark eyes and determination in the angle of his jaw and knew he was as aroused as she. 'Hang on to me.'

He took his hand from her breast and lifted her fingers from his erection to his shoulder. Instinctively she held tight there. Just as well, because her knees threatened to buckle as he returned to caressing her breast, his other hand working between her legs.

Now she moved with every slide of his hand, finding the rhythm and forgetting her inhibitions. This felt so good, so perfect, she...

'Christo!' It was a desperate shout, half-muffled by the wave of ecstasy enveloping her.

She had half a second to see him smile, then he bent his head to hers. His kiss was lavish, demanding yet reassuring, connecting them even as she shattered, her soul shooting towards the heavens as her body shuddered and almost collapsed.

Christo took her weight, drawing her against him and hugging her tight. His warmth enveloped her and soft words rained down, soothing her gradual descent from that acute peak of pleasure.

Finally the shudders became random trembles and the burning white light dissipated as she clung to him, limp with satiation. Dimly Emma wondered that she felt no embarrassment at climaxing in front of him. She'd imagined finding release with Christo in bed with the lights off, not flaunting her pleasure before him. But it had felt perfect.

'Thank you. That was...'

Emma couldn't find the right words so gave up. Instead she smiled against his muscled chest and let herself sag in his arms, knowing he had her.

His erection hard against her belly reminded her that Christo hadn't found satisfaction. She wanted him to enjoy what she had and slid her hand between them.

'Not yet, *glyka mou*. Let's get you somewhere comfortable.' He stepped clear of his clothes, then scooped her up in his arms.

Emma's eyes snapped open and she fell into his slate-blue gaze. Was that satisfaction she saw? Or anticipation?

As he laid her on the bed a shiver shot through her at the prospect of what lay ahead. Still languid from that intense orgasm, she felt a scurry of nerves as Christo opened a nearby drawer then rolled on a condom.

'I haven't done this before.' The words jerked out of her and she licked her lips, torn between fascination, eagerness and just a touch of apprehension.

He paused, kneeling on the bed, arms braced beside her. Something flared in his eyes, something she couldn't decipher. 'But you want to?'

It was the second time he'd asked. It struck her that, far from being the domineering, macho bully she'd pegged him for when he'd made that demand about her living as his wife, Christo was careful with her. The tension riding his bunched shoulders and clenched jaw was obvious, but he held back. Did he feel the urgency she'd felt just minutes ago? Her mind boggled at his control.

Emma lifted her hand towards him and nodded. 'Show me how to make it good for you.'

Zeus preserve him. How to make it good for him!

Christo grimaced. 'It's already far too good.' He'd been so close to the brink that, even when he'd removed her hand, he'd almost come just watching and feeling her climax. And when she'd snuggled into him like a living blanket…

'But it could be better.' Her eyes were enormous but he read that obstinate mouth and felt his own curve.

'Oh, definitely.' He moved to straddle her legs, getting high just from the sight of her lithe, beautiful body laid out for his enjoyment.

Christo wanted Emma badly. He needed to possess her, fill her and claim her as his own. The urge to spread her legs and take her was so strong. But she was a virgin. He had no experience of virgins but he knew he needed to make this as easy for her as possible.

Instead of pushing her legs apart, he bent and pressed a light kiss to her hip bone. She jolted, as if still wired from her orgasm. The scent of feminine arousal wafted to him and he smiled. He'd give her a first time she'd never forget.

With that silent vow, Christo set about learning her body.

Emma protested. In between her sighs and gasps as he found a particularly sensitive spot to kiss or lick or stroke. He discovered a place at her ankle that undid her. A spot near the small of her back. Her inner elbow where he'd driven her to the edge that night on Corfu. And the more obvious places. Her breasts that filled his palms so sweetly. The sweep from neck to shoulder. And her inner thighs. By the time he'd finished she was trembling with need and he felt as if he'd been forged from pure, burning steel.

When he nudged his knee between her legs they fell open instantly and elation surged. He'd waited so long. He braced himself on one arm and, sliding his other hand beneath her, tilted her.

Blazing eyes met his. 'Finally!'

'Don't tell me you didn't enjoy yourself.' His mouth rucked up at one side at the memory of exactly how much Emma had enjoyed his caresses. Her skin was flushed and there was a dreamy look in her eyes that contradicted her attempt at brusqueness.

'It was wonderful.' She sighed. 'But I want *you*.'

Strange how her words reverberated within him. How long had he wanted to hear that? Emma wanting him, not running or fighting him.

Her fingers curled around him and his breath hissed. He'd done his best to prepare her but, at her touch, he could hold back no longer.

Christo leaned in, letting her guide him till he was positioned at her slick entrance. She gave a little wriggle at the contact and he rolled his eyes. He was never going to last; that was a given.

'Lift your knees.' His voice was as rough as gravel, but she understood, and he felt her legs lift to cradle his hips. He pressed into the most exquisite, firm heat. His breath stalled and he had to fight not to pump hard. Instead he kept his eyes on Emma and saw her brow wrinkle, as if in confusion.

'Okay?'

She blinked up at him but he saw no sign of pain. 'Odd but okay.'

'Odd?' He shook his head as he allowed himself to slip a little further. The sensations were overwhelming now. The feel of Emma taking him was so good Christo shook with the effort of restraint.

A soft hand touched his face. 'Are you all right?'

Christo grimaced. 'That's my line.' Clearly he wasn't doing this right if Emma felt nothing but concern for him.

Lifting one hand, he cupped her breast then bent to lower his head and suck at her nipple.

'Ah!' She lifted off the bed, drawing him further into that enticing heat. Fingernails dug into his shoulders as he caressed her and inexorably drove home.

Christo lifted his head and read Emma's glazed eyes. No pain there, no fear, just the same wonder he felt as he withdrew and forged home again.

With slow deliberation, Christo set a pace that had her rocking against him. Then, as she licked her lips and said his name, he reached his limit. Christo felt the bunch of tightening muscles in his arms, legs and backside. His rhythm changed, became urgent and inescapable, and the tingling began, racing down his spine and round to his groin.

There was just time to recognise the convulsive clasp of

Emma's tight muscles around him when rapture slammed into him, a rolling tidal wave that went on and on. She curled up, her climaxing body jerking and trembling in unison with his.

Blindly he dropped to one elbow, protectively scooping her close as together they plunged off the edge into oblivion.

CHAPTER ELEVEN

EMMA WOKE TO a sense of luxury and warmth. She lay, savouring the feeling of wellbeing. Opening her eyes, she discovered it was early morning, pale, rosy light spilling through the open window.

She was in Christo's bed.

Unreadable eyes watched her and she discovered that luscious sense of comfort came from the fact she was cuddled against him, lying on her side with one knee hooked over his hip and his arms around her.

'How are you?' His words caressed her mouth and, strangely, that seemed almost as intimate as the way their lower bodies were aligned, his powerful erection a reminder of what they'd shared last night.

Her face flushed. Even her ears tingled. What they'd shared went beyond everything she'd imagined.

'Fantastic.'

His mouth crooked at one corner. 'You are that.' Then dark eyebrows angled down. 'Not hurting at all?'

'I don't think so.' Emma shifted slightly, registering a slight heaviness between her legs, more an awareness than anything.

It wasn't any change in her body that concerned her. It was the consequence of sharing Christo's bed.

She couldn't pretend any more that he was a despicable monster. Yet was sex any solution to their convoluted relationship?

'So you got your wedding night after all. Just as you specified in the contract.' What made her say it, Emma didn't know. Except belatedly she realised she didn't have a clue where they went from here.

That hint of a smile vanished in an instant.

Christo's muscles stiffened around her. 'You're saying last night was about the contract? Giving yourself for a piece of property?' The abrupt change in him was shocking, his tone scathing.

'It was you who insisted I owed you a night in your bed!' Emma pushed against that solid chest and reared back, but he kept her where she was. Close enough to read, for a second, what seemed like disappointment in those smoky eyes.

She stilled, intrigued, telling herself it couldn't be. Christo wore that look again, the steely one that spoke of severe disapproval. His mouth was tight and the pulse at his temple drummed too fast. Yet still there was something in his eyes…

'Why did you sleep with me, then?' she challenged, her throat tight. 'Because I *owed* you? Was I some trophy? Was last night payback for me leaving you?'

'You think I collected a debt for pride's sake?' Christo's nostrils flared. 'I slept with you because you drive me crazy with wanting.' The words carried the lash of accusation. As if he held her responsible. 'Because there's a connection between us. You felt it too. Don't tell me you didn't.' He drew in a deep breath. 'Last night was about you and me, nothing else.'

Emma's breath jammed in her lungs. She couldn't doubt his sincerity, not when she was so close she read every change in his body.

'Why did you come to my bed, Emma?' The look in his eyes told her the answer was important to him.

She didn't want to reply but what was the point in trying to hide the truth?

'I couldn't fight myself any more,' she finally admitted. 'You're right. There *is* a connection.' It was growing stronger all the time. Emma tried to tell herself it was just sex but it was more complicated than that.

'You want to be with me.' He pulled her closer and she let him, because this was where she wanted to be, even if she had no idea where it would lead.

'I do.' She sighed. Once that would have been an admission of defeat. Now it was the simple truth. She was tired of hiding from it.

'And I want to be with you.' He nudged her chin up and she read his sincerity.

Excitement pulsed through her. Whether this was a mistake or not, at least in this they were equals. Emma couldn't find it in herself to turn away from him again.

She shrugged, feeling a little foolish. 'I only mentioned the contract because I'm a bit out of my depth.'

At her words he lifted his hand to stroke her hair back from her face. The gesture was so tender, almost loving. Emma felt a pang of regret that this could never be love. But she was an adult. She'd accept reality. Take the pleasure they both wanted and move on when it ended.

'I'm sorry. I overreacted.' Christo's mouth compressed to a crooked line. 'It's my own fault for spelling it out on paper. That *was* hurt pride.' Emma blinked at the admission and the apology. More and more, the Christo Karides she'd despised was transforming into a man she liked.

Emma nestled against that solid chest, inhaling his rich, salty male scent. After just one night she feared she was addicted to his body. His hugs banished the loneliness she'd felt since Papou's death. But it wasn't only that. In Christo's arms she felt wanted, cherished.

'It's a hot button of mine,' he continued. 'Women who trade their bodies for gain.'

'I suppose you've met a few, being rich.' And handsome.

'Enough.' Then, to her surprise, he went on. 'My mother was like that. She married my father for his money.'

Emma pulled back, searching Christo's face. Behind the scowl she was sure she saw hurt. It made her insides twist.

'Are you sure? Maybe she just—'

'No mistake.' Slate-blue eyes held hers. 'My father was good-looking and successful but he didn't have a loving nature.' Again that quirk of Christo's lips that looked more like pain than amusement. 'He had an eye for stunning women and my mother was a beauty queen. They married because she got pregnant with me.' Christo shook his head. 'He was a hard man, but honourable and faithful, whereas her main interest was spending. She admitted she'd never wanted me. Pregnancy was just her way to secure her future.'

'That's appalling! How could any mother say that to her child?' The thought sickened Emma.

Christo shrugged. 'She was furious at the time. She blamed me for my father finding out she'd cheated on him.' At Emma's questioning look, he added, 'I walked in on her with her lover and didn't react well. My father eventually heard about the fuss, I assume from the staff.'

Emma tried to imagine what it would be like, discovering your parent with a lover. She wondered what Christo meant by her not reacting well but, given the stark line of his clamped jaw, thought it best not to ask.

'So she spoke in the heat of the moment.' Emma didn't like the sound of Christo's mother but she hated seeing the lines of pain bracketing his mouth when he spoke of her.

'You're trying to excuse her? Don't bother. She never spoke to me after that. I haven't seen her since. She's living in Brazil now, married to a mining magnate, probably pretending she doesn't have an adult son.'

Emma digested that in silence. With a mother like that, and a father he'd described as hard, Christo began to make more sense. He was an only child and love had clearly been in short supply in his family. She wondered with a pang if he'd ever had tenderness from his father. Or anything approaching a happy family life.

Was it surprising he'd held back from Anthea, admitting he didn't have the skills to care for a child? There was even a lop-sided logic to his plan to acquire a convenient bride to fill that role, if he had no experience of a loving family.

What mattered, she realised, was that he hadn't shirked his responsibility. He was determined to make a good home for Anthea. She couldn't fault him for that.

Honourable, he'd called his father. Surely Christo had inherited that trait, or at least a strong sense of responsibility?

Emma surveyed him under her lashes. He could be a hard man. Look at the way he'd set about acquiring a wife. But there was more to him. Christo felt deeply. That was clear from everything she saw in his face and from the tightly contained voice as he'd relayed that horrible story about his mother. Obviously he held back a dam of painful emotions.

He didn't just feel responsible for his niece, either. He cared for her, even if he was just learning how to express it. That was why the sight of them bonding had fascinated Emma. It was as if he got as much out of being with Anthea as she did.

Plus, he cared for Emma. Last night at the reception he'd smoothed her way, ensuring she was at ease. His smiles and laughter had been genuine. She'd *liked* him as well as desired him. Then there was the way he'd taken time to ensure her first experience of sex was spectacular. Emma knew that wasn't always the case. Christo had put her needs above his own.

Perhaps the man she'd fallen for in Australia hadn't been a total mirage. Christo Karides was more complex than she'd credited.

'What are you thinking about?'

His words drew her attention back to his face. Their eyes meshed and heat simmered beneath her skin. How could he do that with just a look?

She shifted, the movement making her breathtakingly aware that she was still wrapped in his arms, naked, her lower body coming up against Christo's erection.

She saw his pulse throb at the contact. The simmer became a scorching blaze, running like wildfire along her veins and over her skin.

'I was thinking you're not the man I imagined you were.'

'Really?' His eyebrows rose, his body tensing.

'There's more to you than I thought,' Emma admitted. 'More to like.'

Christo's features eased and the corner of his mouth curled up. 'You certainly seemed to like me well enough last night,' he murmured in a drawl that dragged through her body like fingers ruffling velvet. She felt a tremor ripple through her belly.

One large hand traced an arabesque along her spine, slowing as it drew low towards her buttocks. Emma's breath stilled as her body thrummed into needy awareness.

'I did, didn't I?' Her voice was husky.

'And *I* like *you*.'

Emma swallowed hard. The words weren't fancy. Yet the way he said them, teamed with the way he looked at her, made them sound like something profound. Something significant.

For a second anxiety gripped her. She'd vowed not to fall for romantic fantasy again. Except this was no extravagant, gilded compliment designed to turn her head. This was plain and unvarnished...and she believed him.

There was tenderness in his touch and in his expression, as well as a good dollop of anticipation. An anticipation she shared.

Mutual attraction was simple and straightforward. She just had to remain clear-headed. Never again would she make the mistake of imagining there was love between them.

'So,' he murmured, 'If you like me and I like you...'

That roving hand palmed her bottom and tugged her flush against him. Emma's breath snagged as his rigid length slid up against that needy spot between her legs. Automatically she curved closer, seeking more.

'Then maybe,' she finished for him, 'we should spend more time together.' On the final word he nudged so close, she felt her flesh part to accommodate him.

Emma's eyes widened at how easy it was and how very, very good. She was just wrapping her fingers around his shoulder to pull even herself closer when Christo shook his head, a grimace, as if of pain, tugging at his mouth.

'Wait.'

Then he was gone, turning away for a condom, leaving her shocked to the core that she hadn't thought about protection. Giving herself to her husband was becoming the easiest thing in the world.

Emma chewed on that fact, wondering what heartache that boded for the future.

It wasn't just heat building inside her. She told herself it was arousal, hunger for the magic he'd shared with her last night. Emma blocked her mind to the possibility it might be anything more.

Then Christo was back, wrapping her close, meeting her eyes with a blazing look that banished all doubts. It was, she decided, time to quit worrying and go with the flow.

He smiled and it was like a light going on in the darkness. The radiance mesmerised her.

'Now, about spending more time together. I have a plan to bring us *very* close together.'

'You do?' Her voice was breathless. For his hand was already skimming her thigh, urging her to lift her knee higher over his waist.

The action spread her open against his groin where furnace-like heat beckoned. Emma shuffled closer and the friction of their bodies aligning sent a zap of energy to every sense receptor. He bumped his hips forward and her breath stopped.

'That feels so good.'

'We haven't even started yet.' The devil was in his eyes as he rubbed against her. Then he claimed her mouth in a slow, sultry, seductive kiss that led to a world of bliss. And from there to a whole morning spent in his arms and a haze of delicious wellbeing.

The haze lingered.

For four days they stayed in Athens, satisfying the public hunger for sightings of Greece's favourite billionaire and his new bride.

It wasn't as difficult as Emma had expected. Christo made everything easy, diverting her when she felt nervous, introducing her to people who were genuinely pleasant and interesting. Never leaving her side. She grew accustomed to the weight of his arm around her waist, or his long fingers threaded through hers, as if it were the most natural thing in the world.

As if her husband enjoyed touching her as much as she delighted in his touch.

They mingled with the rich and famous at exclusive restaurants, a gala gallery opening and a couple of parties. They had cocktails on the luxury yacht of an Italian billionaire who was interested in Christo's Athens redevelopment plan. Instead of leaving her to talk business with their host, Christo drew her in and mentioned that the property in question had been owned by her family for years. That she had a commercial interest in it. Emma had been stunned by the acknowledgement, feeling a flush of satisfaction and pride that her Papou's far-sighted purchase was now to be the centrepiece of a significant development.

She felt almost sophisticated in a daring designer outfit of white silk trousers and a vibrant red top with a deeply slashed V down the back that Christo couldn't resist. As they stood talking to their host, Christo kept running his fingers down her bare skin, making her tingle all over.

A week earlier she'd have thought he was doing it for the benefit of the paparazzi who were settled in small boats with telephoto lenses trained on the cruiser.

Now she knew better. For if Christo was attentive in public it was nothing to what he was like when they were alone. He was always touching her, always close, always finding new ways to bring her pleasure. She spent all night in his arms. They showered together, ate together, yet the urgent hunger between them grew more, not less, intense.

It was as if, that first night in Athens, they'd pulled down the barriers to reveal a need that couldn't be assuaged. Each day it increased. As if this were a proper marriage and they really were honeymooners.

When Emma let slip that despite her stop-overs in Athens she'd never visited the Acropolis, Christo arranged a special tour. One of the site's archaeological experts guided them around the ancient hilltop on their final afternoon. It was a wonderful experience. Even the throng of tourists, some of whom were as interested in her and Christo as in the marble temples, didn't detract from it.

Standing at the perimeter wall—watching the sunset wash the city apricot, gold then finally deep violet, as their guide told them tales of long ago—Christo pulled her back against his powerful frame, arms wrapped around her, his breath stroking her hair.

Emma felt such contentment, such joy, that for a moment it frightened her. Until she remembered she was taking one day at a time. That what they shared was based on desire, not love, and as such it couldn't last.

Strange that the knowledge wasn't as comforting as before.

CHAPTER TWELVE

THREE WEEKS AFTER their time together in Athens and things were excellent. Satisfaction filled Christo as he strode from the car park towards the old part of Corfu Town.

Anthea was growing into a happy kid instead of an apprehensive one. She adored Emma who, far from keeping her distance with a stranger's child, gave her all the warmth and encouragement she craved. Pleasure filled him, thinking of the pair together. He couldn't have asked for more.

The nanny's recent resignation on the grounds that life at the villa was too quiet was a relief. Her play for his attention still rankled. Now he had to secure a new carer but meanwhile Dora's niece filled the role admirably.

There'd been no more innuendo in the world's press about a runaway bride. Instead he and Emma had been dubbed the world's most besotted newlyweds.

Business proceeded on schedule with none of the expected negative fallout. Actually, there was more potential investor interest in his latest project than before, thanks to the Athens publicity. His bride had been a massive hit.

And the fireworks between him and Emma were now only of the sexual sort. No more flare-ups of indignation or accusation.

Heat smote his belly. Emma was so passionate, so eager.

The one thing that surprised him was how their intimacy wasn't confined to sex. It simmered between them, as if some invisible filament bound them together—their bodies but also their minds, their thoughts, even their amusement at the same things.

Christo slung his jacket over his shoulder and quickened his step through the late-afternoon throng. Emma wasn't expecting him and he looked forward to her welcome. Sex was phenomenal with his virgin bride, a quick learner who drove him to the brink with a mere touch. But just as alluring was the way her hazel eyes widened with delight whenever she saw him. Then they glittered more green than brown, a sign, he'd learned, that she was excited or happy.

Making Emma happy was fast becoming one of his favourite things.

He strode along the Liston, the wide, marble-paved pedestrian street edging the old town. On one side graceful colonnaded buildings lined the road, housing restaurants. On the other, the restaurants' shady outdoor seating gave onto the park with its unexpected cricket pitch, a quirk dating from the years of British rule. There was an elegance to the beautiful street, now full of promenading visitors, locals and waiters hurrying past with loaded trays. But he didn't have time to linger. He was here to find his wife.

As usual the word 'wife' stirred a zap of anticipation.

He'd left Athens a day early, arriving in Corfu on Thursday, because after four days of long hours in Athens he wanted Emma.

Once the idea of rearranging his schedule to be with a woman would have perturbed him. Now he viewed it as a perk of marriage. He had a desirable wife. Why wouldn't he spend time with her? He was CEO, after all. Careful planning, a couple of extra-long days and a little delegation meant everything was under control.

He turned left into one of the narrow lanes that snaked between tall Venetian-style buildings with their pastel colours and long shutters. Small shops did a brisk trade and he dodged souvenir hunters and families with ice-creams, delighted at the anonymity he found so hard to achieve in Athens.

Since his youth Christo's actions had been reported and scrutinised. He'd spent his life carrying the weight of expectation, first of his demanding father, then of the business world and, latterly, the public with its unending appetite for gossip about the rich and famous.

Maybe that was why he liked this island so much. With a few precautions he was generally free to do as he liked.

Right now he liked the idea of surprising his wife.

Consulting his phone, he took a turning, then another, passing a small square with a tiny church and a vibrant burst of pink bougainvillea shading patrons at a café. Another turn and...

Christo pulled up mid-stride.

His breath hissed between his teeth as a phantom fist landed a punch to his gut. He rocked back then found his balance in the wide-set stance of a man ready to defend what was his.

For there was Emma, hair high in an elegant style that left her slender, sexy neck bare. She wore one of her new outfits, cream trousers that clung to the curves of her rump and hips before falling loosely to jewelled sandals that exactly matched the amber of her sleeveless top.

She looked delicious enough to sink his teeth into. But Christo's attention zeroed in on the man with her. The man standing too close, his hand on her arm, his smiling face bent towards her.

Emma didn't mind. She smiled and nodded, listening as he leaned in to murmur in her ear.

Christo surged forward, ignoring the strange sensation, as if both his lungs and his throat constricted.

A bevy of chattering teenagers came in from a side-street, impeding his progress. By the time he reached the doorway where Emma had stood, the guy was gone and she was a glow of colour further ahead.

Impatient, he strode to catch up with her, his hand curling around her elbow.

'Christo! What are you doing here?'

Watching the excited green spark in her eyes, basking in the warmth of her smile, the fierce blaze in his belly dimmed and he found himself smiling back.

'Looking for you.' Her soft skin felt so good. Her lush honey scent was rich as nectar.

Christo's chest filled with a wild riot of feelings. He recognised pleasure and relief and refused to go further. Yet even a man committed to avoiding extreme emotion registered the depth of his relief.

Had he been *scared* Emma was more interested in the stranger than him? It didn't take a psychologist to read the scars of his mother's behaviour there.

To Emma he'd implied he hadn't known about his mother's betrayal till the end. Actually, he'd known most of his life. It was only when he'd found her with a teenager from his own high school, just two years older than himself, that Christo had finally cracked. There'd been no hiding from his father the smashed furniture or his bruised knuckles as he'd taken the other guy down. His mother had hated him for that and his father had withdrawn even further.

Christo had learned not to trust women, even when they came at a high price. Not to expect love or even companionship. He'd thought of a wife only as an asset, a commodity.

Looking into Emma's open features and the genuine smile curling her lips, Christo had a revelation.

He didn't want it to be that way.

The chains of the past were too restrictive. He wanted...

The idea of what he wanted stunned him.

'Where are we going?' Emma couldn't suppress the smile that kept breaking out. She'd missed Christo ever since he'd left for Athens on Monday morning. Here he was, back early.

For her? A shiver of excitement tugged through her belly and she strove to suppress it.

'Somewhere we can talk.' He threaded a way through the maze of alleys, emerging on the road behind the neo-classical Palace of St Michael and St George. Minutes later they descended a ramp built into the city walls to the tiny Faleraki beach.

It was one of her favourite places. Quiet and cut off from the bustle, the little bay looked across the water to the city ramparts, the towering Old Fortress, and beneath it the marina packed with yachts. Further down the beach a ramshackle pier provided a platform for local kids who were fooling around and jumping into the depths.

Christo led her to the point at the end of the small beach and the outdoor café. Unsurprisingly, a waiter emerged in-stantly, leading them to a shaded spot apart from other ta-bles. It was the sort of thing that happened all the time with Christo, whether because they recognised his face or read him as a man who expected and happily paid for the best.

Instead of a table, they were installed on a comfortable couch under a wide umbrella. Their cool drinks and a plat-ter of food arrived minutes later, set on the glass coffee table beyond which the aquamarine shallows gave way to deeper water the colour of lapis lazuli.

Emma sighed and sank back into the cushioned seat. She could get used to this.

Just as she'd grown used to the warmth of Christo's hand enfolding hers and the buzz of delight she got when he looked at her as if she were special. Those eyes…

Her heartbeat stuttered and seemed to pause before stumbling back into rhythm.

No. She wouldn't allow flights of fancy. This charge of excitement, like his heated expression, was about desire, attraction and physical pleasure. Nothing more.

'What brought you back from Athens?' He shrugged, those powerful shoulders riding high. Still he held her hand and it struck her that his expression was different, more guarded than she'd seen it in weeks. 'Is everything all right? Are you okay?'

She sensed something had changed. Something important.

His response proved her too fanciful. 'Everything's perfect. Just as it should be.' He leaned across to add ice to his ouzo, watching it cloud. 'I simply felt like taking a long weekend.'

Christo turned, lifting his glass. Automatically Emma raised her glass of tangy local ginger beer.

Yia mas.' To us. A traditional toast, but when Christo leaned near, with that blazing look in his eyes, Emma felt...

She blanked that thought, wishing she'd ordered a shot of fiery ouzo instead of a soft drink. Something to jerk her out of useless imaginings.

'Who was that man?'

'Sorry?'

'The man you were with.' Emma caught the echo of something hard in Christo's tone, like steel hidden beneath velvet. For a moment she wondered if it could be jealousy. The possibility made something foolish within her swell.

'A local businessman.'

Christo sipped his drink then put it down and turned more fully towards her.

'And his business with you?' There it was again, a hint of sharpness.

Emma was torn between delight and disappointment. Just because Christo was possessive didn't mean anything. She was, for now, his wife. She'd seen how far he'd go to protect the public image of a happy couple.

The bubbling happiness she'd felt since the moment he'd sought her out in the old town faded.

'Emma?' Concern coloured his voice as he took her drink from her fingers then captured that hand too. 'What's wrong? What did he—?'

'Nothing! Nothing's wrong. He didn't do anything.' With a deep breath she pushed aside that silly sense of dissatisfaction and smiled. 'He runs a business decorating and catering for weddings. He interviewed me for a job.'

'A job?' She might have said she was flying to the moon, given his expression of blank surprise.

'Something to use my skills.' And earn an income. She needed funds to get her business off the ground. She didn't want to wait ten months till they went their separate ways and she received money from the Athens project.

'You're bored?'

Emma tilted her head, surveying him. 'I need to work, Christo. The villa is lovely and I have exciting plans to turn it into an exclusive resort. But that's longer term.' At least till she could get money to seed the first stages.

'This man—he offered you a job?'

Emma saw the tight angle of Christo's jaw and hesitated. 'He's consulting his partner first, but he was very positive.'

In fact, his enthusiasm had given Emma pause. The work had sounded good, despite the commuting time from the villa, but he'd been a little too friendly, his personal interest in her obvious. She hadn't really felt comfortable, had already decided...

'I don't want you working for him.'

'Sorry?'

'He's not trustworthy.'

'You know him?' Christo was a stranger to the area.

'I know his type. It wasn't business he had in mind.'

Exactly what Emma had thought. Yet Christo's assertion, implying he had the final say over her actions, stirred indignation. She tugged a hand from his and picked up her glass, taking a long swallow, then putting it down with a click on the table.

'*I* will decide whether or not to take the job.'

The glint in his eyes told her he wanted to disagree. 'You're my wife. You don't need to work.'

Emma arched her eyebrows. 'You're worried what people will think?' She could just about forgive his attempted intervention, given her own concerns about the guy who'd interviewed her. But to be told she couldn't work because of Christo's image...

Christo shook his head. 'I'm not trying to trap you at home. I have nothing against you having a job. I'll help you find one, if you like. I just don't want someone trying to take advantage of you.'

Perhaps that should sound strange coming from the man who'd traded on her besotted naivety to trap her into marriage. Instead it sounded *caring*. Not merely the result of macho possessiveness. There was a good dose of that, judging from the jut of his jaw. But there was more too.

For a second it reminded her of the old days, with her family, and particularly Papou, being over-protective. In the past Emma had found that trying, but she realised it felt good to know someone cared. She'd missed that.

'Emma.' Christo bent closer, as if trying to decipher her thoughts.

'You're not worried the press would say a billionaire's wife shouldn't work?'

A crack of laughter sounded. 'As if that's relevant!' Then, just as suddenly, he turned sombre. 'But I'm serious about that guy. The way he looked at you, he definitely wasn't thinking about work.'

Emma looked into Christo's strikingly handsome face, looking for self-interest, for some hint of manipulation. All she read was concern.

Once more that glow of warmth filled her.

She squeezed the big hand that held hers just a fraction too tight. 'Okay, I'll bear that in mind.' She'd already decided not to take the job, but she didn't want Christo thinking he could order and she'd immediately obey. He was domineering enough without further encouragement.

For long seconds he said nothing. Then he nodded and Emma released a pent-up breath. This felt like a victory. More. It felt like caring and respect.

Deep inside something tight and knotted frayed.

Christo gathered her against him, shifting so they both faced the glorious view. A shoal of fish glinted, turning in the crystalline shallows a few metres away. A yacht appeared around the promontory, its sail pristine white against the deep blue of sea and distant land.

Emma felt the comforting thud of Christo's heart and the warm weight of his arm around her. His breath feathered her hair and she inhaled his unique cedar, leather and spice scent. Elation rose.

'I'm glad to be back on Corfu, Emma.'

She smiled up at him, surprised to hear herself admit, 'I'm glad too.'

'Busy?' The deep voice came from behind Emma next morning as she sat in the courtyard loggia. Warm hands covered her shoulders and slid down her bare arms.

The pencil spilled from her hand onto the table. Her eyelids flickered as tingling heat rushed through her. She breathed deep, inhaling the familiar scent of Christo mingling with the last wisteria blooms. It was a heady mix.

Did he pull her close or did she lean back? Either way, as usual, she melted.

It was less than an hour since she'd left him and a giggling Anthea playing hide and seek in the garden. Two hours since Christo had held Emma pinioned against the wall of the shower, water sluicing over the pair of them, lips soldered together as he'd pumped into her, bringing them both to rapturous completion.

Thinking of it made her nipples peak and awareness tighten her inner muscles.

She sighed as he bent, nuzzled the hair from her neck and grazed his teeth where her neck curved into her shoulder. Emma shuddered. He knew all her sensitive spots.

'You're too distracting. I'm supposed to be working.'

Yesterday's conversation had reminded her how much she still had to do to get her business off the ground. She'd researched the market and competitors, checked local government approval processes and developed a business plan. She'd begun a website, scouted local suppliers and made plans for changes to the villa. But her non-existent cash flow meant she couldn't proceed as fast as she'd like.

Christo lifted his head and Emma bit her tongue rather than voice the protest that rose to her lips.

'On the weekend?'

She opened her mouth to say that was what he did, spent the weekends working, but it was no longer true. Last weekend there'd been a couple of calls to the Italian they'd met in Athens to discuss their joint venture. But that was all.

What had happened to the busy entrepreneur who'd initially seemed out of place at the villa?

'What are the drawings for?' Christo sat beside her at the table, pulling his chair so close his leg brushed hers and her shoulder nudged his upper arm.

She sighed and closed the papers. 'It's a long-term vision for the villa next door. But my main focus right now really needs to be on getting this place ready.'

'You're sure you want to do that?'

'Of course.' She needed the income and she had the skills to make it work. Eventually, when she and Christo divorced, this place would be hers free and clear.

Strange how the thought of being free of Christo no longer held the allure it once had. In fact, it chilled her to the bone despite the morning's warmth.

* * *

Christo had problems with the idea of outsiders here. Security would be a nightmare but, more than that, the place was their private haven. It wasn't modern like his Athens apartment but it felt like home. More than the ostentatious house where he'd grown up ever had.

'You won't mind sharing your home with strangers?'

Christo felt Emma's muscles tighten almost imperceptibly at his words. Yet she'd seemed rapt in the idea when she talked about it before.

Because she needs to support herself. Because you robbed her of the inheritance that should be hers, at least temporarily.

A decent man would give Emma back everything he'd taken.

Christo considered himself decent, if tough. He dismissed a pang of conscience.

'It's either that or move out completely. I'd rather be on hand when there are guests, to deal with their needs.'

'What about your privacy?'

'That's not a luxury I can afford.'

Christo stilled. He felt like a heel. 'Care to show me the drawings for next door?' When Emma hesitated, he reached forward. 'May I?'

She shrugged. 'Why not? Papou bought the neighbouring property, but it needed a lot of work, and he got sick not long afterwards so he never got around to doing anything with it.'

Christo surveyed the drawings. 'You have a good eye,' he murmured, lifting the top page to look at the next and the next. 'This could be something special. Even better than developing this place.'

'You think so?'

He met her stare, noting the excitement in her eyes at

odds with the press of her lips. As if she were scared to expect too much.

'I like the combination of modern and traditional. And extending the outdoor living space next to this—' he pointed '—is it a sunken garden?'

'It is, with a fabulous view over its own cove.'

'It would make a perfect venue for exclusive celebrations.'

'Weddings in particular.' She was enthusiastic now. 'I could lure a lot of people from overseas for a romantic wedding in Greece. Or anniversaries, or private holidays. One day, when I'm solvent, I'll tackle the remodelling.'

'I could help with that. My company specialises in property development.' Though on a much larger scale.

Emma spun round in her seat, her eyes huge. 'You threatened to withdraw your money from my uncle's business unless I stayed married to you. Yet you're *offering* it to me now?'

Not Christo's finest hour. He'd been desperate to convince Emma to stay with him. That need hadn't gone. It was just tempered by other things.

Feelings. It's tempered by what you feel for her. What you want her to feel for you.

Christo's pulse hammered high in his throat. Suddenly he didn't feel as invincible as usual.

'You agreed to my terms and I trust you to keep them,' he said, as if that was all he wanted, her presence for another ten months.

Christo paused, wondering if she had any notion how significant that admission was. Trust didn't come easily to him. Yet he'd discovered in Emma a woman unlike any he'd known. A woman who might disagree with him, but who, he was sure, wouldn't lie. She was sexy and passionate, gentle and emotional, practical and forthright. She cared for orphans and ageing housekeepers and maybe even for him.

Everything within him stilled as he acknowledged how much he wanted that.

'I want you to be happy and fulfilled, Emma.'

His words clearly took her by surprise, despite all they'd shared. But why shouldn't she be surprised? He'd couched their intimacy only in terms of sex. He'd let her imagine their connection was all about desire and satisfying carnal appetites. The truth, he'd discovered, ran far, far deeper.

Still she hesitated.

'Look on it as an advance against the money I owe you from the Athens property.' Not that he intended to use her funds for this. It would be his gift, but she didn't need to know that now.

Emma tilted her head to one side, as if trying to see him better. 'That would virtually dismantle the hold you have over me. You do realise that?'

Christo shrugged as if it were a small thing. As if his heart wasn't pummelling his ribs sickeningly and his neck wasn't prickling at the thought of her slipping away from him. But it wouldn't come to that.

'Until the year's up I still have ultimate say over the property.' He couldn't relinquish total control yet.

Slowly she nodded. But the reminder of that ace up his sleeve didn't dim the wonder in those hazel eyes. Her expression made him glow. As he had when he'd found her yesterday and she'd looked at him with such patent delight.

Had anyone ever looked at him as Emma did? For sure, he'd never felt this way about any other woman.

He lifted his hand to her satiny cheek, brushing it with the back of his knuckle. Something welled high in his chest and he opened his mouth to tell her…

'Emma!' A child's voice rang out and they turned to see Anthea and Dora's niece step out of the house. The new nanny released the girl's hand and predictably she flew across the courtyard to Emma's side like a bullet.

Emma gathered her up, settling her on her lap and nodding as Anthea told her how she'd helped tidy up.

Seeing the two together, the sensation in Christo's chest twisted into something powerful and barely familiar. This was how he'd imagined them, even better than he'd imagined. Yet it wasn't mere satisfaction he experienced.

Abruptly Anthea stopped chattering and turned to him, holding her arms out. 'Cwisto!' Inevitably her lisp made him smile. 'Up, pease. Up!'

It still stunned him that he'd built a rapport with Cassie's daughter. That he hadn't inadvertently hurt her because of his lack of experience. Guilt and the shadow of the past had persuaded him it wouldn't be possible. That he didn't deserve her trust.

Christo looked from Anthea to Emma and absorbed a barrage of emotions. Who'd have believed his world would be upended by two females? One tiny and demanding. The other feisty yet sweet. Both vulnerable. Both adorable.

Emma passed the little girl over to him, and he read in Emma's expression something he hadn't seen before. He wanted to freeze that moment, analyse that look, question her. But Anthea was wriggling, demanding he take her to see the baby birds in the nest they'd found in the garden.

He got up, slanting a look at Emma. But she turned away, folding the plans that riffled in the breeze.

Later, he told himself. This was too important to ignore.

CHAPTER THIRTEEN

'THE PLACE DEFINITELY has excellent potential,' Christo said as they left the empty villa and headed down the path to a private cove, smaller but no less beautiful than theirs next door. With each step their view of the jewel-toned water improved. Drifts of wildflowers, pink, white, blue and yellow, frothed up against the boles of massive olive trees and iconic tall cypresses.

Emma nodded, trying to stifle bubbling excitement that Christo was so positive about the place. All through their inspection Christo had asked tough, insightful questions. He'd closely examined the house and outbuildings which Emma hoped to turn into extra accommodation.

'It would take a lot of money to renovate,' she said. The more they inspected, the more she feared she'd underestimated costs. Emma knew events management but nothing about building. That was Christo's field.

He took her hand, weaving his fingers through hers. Emma's breath stalled then accelerated to a gallop. Ever since Athens he took every chance to touch her, to be close. The attraction between them was real, not manufactured for the press.

Was that why her heart sang when he touched her?

It might not be love but this…fling felt wonderful. As if she'd undone the shackles of grief, self-doubt and anger and had stepped free of them. She felt lighter at heart than she could ever remember.

See? She could enjoy the moment. Take pleasure like a sophisticated adult and…

Christo smiled and her thoughts frayed. He tugged her hand, leading her off the path and onto the deserted crescent of fine sand. Metres away the sun glinted off shallow water that sparkled like gems. It was a private paradise, screened at this end of the beach from open water by a tumble of rocks. There was just the shush of the sea on sand, a songbird in the trees above and Christo.

Yearning trembled through her.

'Marketed right and run well, it would be worth the investment. It can't be left. A vacant property will just degrade. And with this—' he gestured to the private beach '—you're onto a winner.'

Emma nodded, struggling to focus on the property, not on the man. 'I've tried to calculate how much it would cost but I haven't got very far.'

He turned back, his grey-blue eyes snaring hers. 'Leave that to me. I'll get someone onto it.'

'You will?' Was he serious about helping with the place?

'Of course.' He released her fingers and instead wrapped both hands around her waist. 'I'll release the resources so you can remodel. My staff will chase up the best local builders.'

Emma was so stunned it took a second to register what he was doing with his hands. Until air wafted around her torso as he urged her arms up, pulling her top over her head.

'Christo!' She darted a look around the empty beach. 'We can't.' Yet her breathlessness proved she was more excited than outraged. Especially when, with one swift movement, he hauled his shirt over his head and dumped it on the sand.

Emma's heart beat too fast as she took in his muscled body. She'd discovered one of her favourite things was to lay her head on his chest, feeling the strong thud of his heart beneath her ear and listening to it hammer as she flicked his nipple with her tongue, or slid her hand down to squeeze his shaft and tease him till he growled and rolled her beneath him.

No growling now. Christo shucked his shoes and the rest of his clothes while she stood staring. She'd thought herself accustomed to the sight of him, all taut muscle and proud virility. But she'd never seen him under the bright blue sky, stark-naked and mightily aroused.

He looked like some Greek god, perfectly proportioned, formidably sexy and utterly intent. Her body softened in anticipation. Involuntarily her inner muscles squeezed and she felt the slick wetness of arousal.

'Believe me, Emma, we can.'

In seconds he'd undone her bra and tossed it onto his clothes. The sun warmed her bare flesh but it was nothing to the blaze of heat as his gaze licked her. She thrilled at the ardour she read in his face, yet they were outdoors and...

'Don't cover yourself, sweet Emma.' She hadn't realised she'd made to cover her breasts till warm hands shackled her wrists. 'Please? I want to see you. You know we're private here. You can trust me.'

Standing there half-naked, feeling totally exposed, Emma realised she *did* trust her husband. More than she'd once believed possible.

'You want sex on the beach?' Emma felt a ripple of shock. But then, despite weeks of passionate sex, she'd been a virgin just a short time ago. This was still new.

He smiled, and her heart took up Zumba behind her ribs. 'With you, I want sex everywhere.'

Christo's gaze snared hers. Arousal beat hard and low in her pelvis. She told herself this was merely physical. Nothing else, nothing to worry about. Conveniently she silenced the part of her that said this felt like far more than sex.

'If you want,' he added. His hands hung, fisted, by his sides and Emma read tension in the line of his jaw.

He meant it. He'd leave her be if she chose. Contrarily, the realisation conquered her natural reserve. She toed off her sandals, her hands going to the zip of her skirt. Then she paused, one last doubt surfacing.

'If we have sex it's not because you've promised to help refit the villa.' She held his gaze, willing him to believe. 'I'm not like your mother. I don't do sex for money.'

Christo stood unmoving so long, she wondered if she'd said the wrong thing. But how could it be wrong when it was the truth?

Finally he unlocked frozen muscles and shook his head. 'You're nothing like her, Emma. You think I don't know that?'

She lifted her shoulders. 'I don't want any misunderstandings between us.'

'Good.' He stepped so close his erection brushed her skirt and she shivered as need corkscrewed through her lower body. 'Just honesty between us now. That's what I want. And you, sweet Emma. I want you so badly.'

Christo's words set off a chain reaction inside, making internal muscles spasm needily and her heart thrum wildly. 'In that case, I hope you have a condom.'

He did. By the time Emma was naked he was sheathed and she on her back on the warm sand, Christo kneeling like a conquering hero between her legs. His eyes had that glazed look he got when aroused and, when he nudged her, she automatically rose to meet him, the sensation so exquisite, she stifled a cry of delight.

'Don't hold back, *glyka mou*. I like hearing you.'

With a tilt of his hips Christo slowly drove in till she felt him lodged right at her heart. Emma told herself that was impossible, but that was how it felt when he tenderly kissed her on the lips and gently rocked against her, evoking sensations that should be just physical but which felt profoundly emotional too.

Like caring, homecoming, sharing, lo…

Warning bells clamoured and Emma knew she had to

break the spell of his tenderness. It was enough to make her believe in things she shouldn't.

Holding tight to his shoulders, she lifted her head and grazed his ear with her teeth. Then, as he'd said he liked hearing her, she whispered to Christo just what she wanted him to do next.

It was like igniting gunpowder. For a millisecond there was breathless stillness, then he erupted in a surge of powerful energy, driving against her in an erotic rhythm that stole her breath as his hand moved first to her breast, then to the sensitive bud between her legs and…

'Christo!' His name was a hoarse shout over and over again that faded to a gasp as he took her to a peak, then another, shattering with her in a cataclysmic orgasm that engulfed them in rapture.

When she was back in her body, Emma felt filled to the brim, sated and spent yet emotional and needy, blinking back tears of reaction to the most astounding experience of her life. All she knew as she hugged Christo close was that she wanted to stay this way for ever.

Gradually her breathing eased and her heartbeat too. Still she clung tight, absorbing the scent of sweat and sex and maleness, feeling the slippery silk of her lover's skin against her.

Not her lover. Her husband.

Or maybe more.

Her breath tore from her throat.

'Come on, let's wash the sand away.' The deep voice murmured in her ear as Christo moved, ignoring her protest and lifting her into his arms.

The water, though not cold, was chilly enough to shock her into full alertness. He waded into the water, carrying her in his arms, and Emma clung to him as if she hadn't spent her childhood swimming several times a week. She didn't want to think about why she felt so needy.

Later, as they lay sprawled on flat rocks at the end of the beach drying in the sun, Emma found herself doing what she'd told herself she wouldn't—seeking more from Christo.

It wasn't his money she wanted and, while he made her feel like a goddess when he took her in his arms and made love to her, Emma wanted to understand him.

Because she loved him.

She'd tried to stifle the knowledge but it wouldn't be silenced any more. She'd told herself it was just sex between them, sex and a business arrangement. But she'd deluded herself. The Christo she'd discovered in Greece was the same man she'd fallen for in Australia. It was only the aberration of the loveless marriage that didn't fit the man she'd come to know and like all over again.

Except, after having heard him describe his parents, she had an inkling about how he could separate love and marriage.

Unfortunately she couldn't do that and the realisation terrified her. Was she fooling herself again, tumbling into love with this man? Did she really know him or did she only think so?

And, if she did, what did she do next?

'Tell me about Cassie.'

'Sorry?' Christo opened one eye and squinted down at the damp honey-brown hair on his chest where Emma rested her head. He enjoyed the feel of her there, her body soft against him, one thigh over his so the intimate heat between her legs was tantalisingly close.

'I wondered about your stepsister.'

Christo frowned. 'Why?'

Emma lifted her head, her palm on his chest. Her eyes were sombre. As if, while he'd been lazing on a cloud of wellbeing, she'd been in a bleaker place altogether.

'*Glyka mou!* What's wrong?' Concern rose instantly.

She shook her head. 'Nothing. I was just thinking…' She shrugged then looked at him almost defiantly. 'How much I don't know about you. You never mention Cassie. But I feel she was important to you.'

Christo stared, stunned at the woman who, once again, turned his world upside down. Any other lover would be snuggled bonelessly against him, enjoying the comedown from that amazing high they'd shared. But not his Emma.

Why was he surprised? Emma was unlike any other woman.

'You said we'd be honest with each other.'

'That doesn't mean I want you prying into ancient history.'

'I see.' She didn't pull away but her luscious body stiffened. Her eyes grew shuttered, no longer reflecting the green of the sea but turning a flat, muddy brown. She turned her head away and guilt stirred in his gullet. He should have tempered his response, not barked at her because she'd touched on what he hated to think about.

Christo's heart thumped as he waited for Emma to roll away but she simply subsided where she'd been. Though the way she held herself reminded him of an animal nursing a wound, stillness betraying pain.

He lifted a hand to stroke her, then stopped.

Christo had spent half a lifetime not thinking about this. He baulked at opening up the past. Yet this was the first time Emma had asked him for anything.

Except a divorce.

He huffed an amused breath at the memory of her breathing fire as she'd demanded he release her from their marriage. She'd been so outrageously, provocatively sexy. At that moment he'd thought he'd die if he didn't have her.

Just as suddenly Christo's amusement faded.

He had her for now. But for how long? He wanted her

permanently, and not because of Anthea or words on a legal document. He just…wanted her for himself.

He dropped his hand to her hair, feeling the suck of her indrawn breath against his chest. For some obscure reason, this mattered to her.

And since Emma mattered to him…

Christo turned his head, his gaze drifting across the blue-green sea.

'She was eleven or twelve when she came to the house. A shy little thing with freckles, plaits and the biggest brown eyes you've ever seen.' Eyes just like Anthea's.

Against his chest Emma stirred but said nothing.

'My father and his second wife had just returned from their honeymoon. Cassie had stayed with relatives in the States while they travelled.'

'How old were you?'

'Almost eighteen.' Two years older than when he'd discovered his mother with her teenage lover. At eighteen Christo had worked in the family business and studied, living up to his father's demand that he excel at both.

'You really only met her once?'

'For a weekend. She arrived on Friday and left on Sunday.' Christo swallowed, the action hurting, as if something sharp had lodged in his throat.

Emma sat up. 'Christo? What's wrong?'

He jerked his gaze round to her, biting the urge to say *he* was wrong.

Get a grip, Karides.

He levered himself up to sit, draping his arms over his knees. 'Nothing. It's okay.'

Was he reassuring himself or her? Despite the sun, his nape prickled with cold.

'She was shy, even with her own mother, and with my father…' He shook his head. 'I think I mentioned he was a tough man. He hadn't a sentimental bone in his body. As for being kind to little girls...

'She tried to avoid him as much as possible and I helped her.'

He'd felt sorry for the kid, given her mother had seemed more concerned about placating her new husband than helping her daughter acclimatise to a new country and a new family. Christo, used to being alone, had been charmed by Cassie's hesitant smiles and shy interest. For the first time in his life, he'd felt he could make a difference.

There was a terrible irony there, if only he'd known.

'I took her swimming and sailing.' Getting her out of his father's way. 'And she used to watch me draw. She found my cartoons amusing.' That, if only he'd realised, had been his worst mistake. His father was annoyed enough at him 'wasting' his time with Cassie, but to have her encourage his scribbling wasn't to be borne. The old man viewed his interest in art with suspicion, a sign of weakness in his heir, who had to be tough and ruthlessly efficient. Real men didn't draw or play games. They closed deals, kept a tight rein on business and took hard decisions.

'She must have enjoyed being with you.'

Christo nodded. 'Yes. She even laughed, when she thought my father wasn't around.' He noticed a pebble on the rock at his feet and threw it, watching it arc over the water, then disappear as if it had never been.

Just like Cassie.

'But my father noticed.' Christo found another pebble and threw it. 'He was concerned about me. Apparently, with my stepsister I was soft and lacking seriousness. He was trying to make a man of me. Not someone who frittered away his time playing games or being sentimental over a kid.'

'I don't think I'd have liked your father.'

Christo turned to see Emma sitting, arms wrapped around her legs, chin resting on her knees. Even scowling she made his pulse quicken.

'He was moulding me so I could face whatever the commercial world threw at me. He lost his own father early and didn't want me struggling as he had.'

Emma's eyes met his and something thumped deep in his chest. 'The world isn't just commerce. There's love and friendship and family.'

Not as far as his father had been concerned. 'The upshot was he decided Cassie wasn't a good influence.'

'But she was only a little girl!' Emma's gaze widened.

Christo spread his hands. 'He felt I wasn't acting like a man.'

That had cut deep, especially as Christo had spent his life living up to his father's expectations.

'There's nothing manly about making a little kid feel alone and scared.'

Christo nodded. 'I agree. But he didn't see it that way. He'd never been one for close relationships. His marriages were about possessing beautiful women who enhanced his kudos.' He paused. 'Anyway, he decided Cassie couldn't stay. She was shipped back to relatives in the States.'

Emma looked aghast. 'Just because you'd been nice to her?'

At last she understood. 'Because I had to be tough. He wouldn't allow anything else and I…' Christo sighed and looked away '…accepted that.' Which made it even worse. 'So she went to America and I never heard from her again. After a while, I forgot about her. Occasionally I'd wonder what she was doing but I never followed up.' Bitterness was sharp on his tongue. 'So I didn't know the relatives who took her in later decided they didn't want another kid to look after. She ended up in foster care, shunted from one place to another.'

'It wasn't your fault.' Emma's whisper slid through him like the serpent in Eden, so tempting.

'Because of me she was banished to live her life with people who didn't want her. Meanwhile, I got on with *my* life as if she didn't matter at all.'

Christo threw another stone out into the water with such force, he almost wrenched his shoulder. 'If I'd done the honourable thing, if I'd bothered to check up on her, things might have turned out differently. She might still be alive.' He dragged in air to fill tight lungs. 'But I'm stronger now. I didn't do right by Cassie, but you can be sure I *will* do my duty by her daughter.'

Emma curled her arms tight around her knees and stared out to sea. Beside her Christo did the same, clearly not wanting to talk further.

Who'd have thought a simple question about his step-sister would reveal so much? Combined with what he'd told her before, it painted a picture that made her heart lurch with sympathy and pain. It was even worse than she'd thought.

A cold, controlling father and a distant, self-absorbed mother. His family hadn't been a family at all. It was remarkable they'd produced a man with as much decency as Christo.

Emma had heard his self-reproach as he'd spoken of Cassie. As if he, as a teenager, could have gone against the girl's mother and stepfather to provide a home for her.

Who'd provided a home for him?

He spoke of doing the honourable thing and about duty. Was that what drove Christo? Emma recalled his words when he'd found her in Corfu. About giving her his name and his word, as if that pledge was more important than love.

Which made sense for a man who didn't know love at all.

For a man who possibly never would.

The experts said what you experienced as a child coloured your character for life. That lack of caring in a child's life stunted their emotional growth.

Emma's abdominal muscles spasmed as the pain intensified. She'd convinced herself she was over Christo, that she could enjoy uncomplicated sex then move on. But she'd given her heart to him in Australia and hadn't stopped loving him, despite anger and disillusionment.

Contrary to what she'd told herself, she'd secretly hoped Christo would come to love her. She'd taken his kindness, passion and ability to make her feel special as signs he'd begun to feel for her what she did for him.

Emma gritted her teeth as the pain settled into a cold, hard ache in her belly and chest.

She'd thought he was softening towards her. That they'd shared more than sex. There'd been companionship and caring, humour, a sense that they were building something together.

In a flash of blinding clarity she realised she'd seen what she wanted to see.

Christo was driven by an unshakeable sense of duty. It was there in his determination to care for his step-niece. To look to the needs of Dora, of all his staff, and Emma too.

No matter how much she admired him for the honourable man he'd become despite the odds, duty was no replacement for love.

She shut her eyes and pictured him with Anthea, remembering his hesitation. True, his wariness was easing, and hopefully that relationship would blossom even more.

But Emma couldn't expect miracles. A man driven by duty, who had no experience of love, would never give her what she needed.

They'd found common ground but that was based on sex. Everything, even his desire to be here on the island, hinged on that and his need to portray the fiction of a happy family to the watching world.

Look at the way he'd snapped at her question about Cassie. Christo hated sharing anything personal. Her status as his wife didn't give her special privileges there.

Her husband was as likely to fall in love with her as snow falling in summer.

Even if theoretically it were possible, could she live with him in a one-sided relationship for the rest of the year, hoping for a miracle?

Emma had never thought of herself as greedy. Yet the idea of giving her all to the man she loved, knowing he felt only a sense of responsibility and lust for her, made her crumple inside.

What if the lust faded? What if someone else caught his eye? That was likely given the glamorous circles he moved in. Emma knew part of the reason he desired her was because she was a novelty to him. Despite the makeover in Athens, she wasn't cut out for his world.

With a hiss of indrawn air Emma shot to her feet. Seconds later she was stumbling across the sand to the scatter of discarded clothes.

'Emma? What's wrong?'

She swayed, struck by a blow of need so strong it almost felled her. The perverse, futile need to turn around and run straight back to Christo.

But what would that achieve? She needed distance. Time to think, to sort out her head and her heart.

'I've just remembered...something.' She grabbed the froth of her cotton lace skirt and stepped into it, yanking up the zip. 'I need to get back to the villa.' Her head spun uselessly as she tried to come up with an excuse. 'There's something I need to do.'

'What is it?'

He was behind her, so close his breath kissed her bare

neck and hair as she wrestled with her clothes. She forced herself to take a deep breath and drag the top on, feeling the material abrade her nipples. But she didn't have time for a bra. She had to get away.

A warm hand closed on her elbow and she jumped so violently, he let go. But now he was before her, those penetrating eyes concerned. It was a terrible temptation to think she was wrong. That maybe Christo did feel...

Emma reared back. Her lovesick heart wanted to believe in a happy ending when she *knew*, when he'd already spelled it out as clearly as he could, that he only wanted sex, and stability for his niece. She'd already fallen for wishful thinking once. She knew better now.

He stood before her, naked and powerfully built, and her longing was so great she had to avert her eyes.

'Talk to me, Emma.' His voice was warm velvet, enfolding her.

She stepped back, almost tripping over a sandal. 'Not now. I have to go—'

'I'm not letting you go anywhere when you're clearly upset.' He crossed his arms over that powerful chest, the picture of masculine obstinacy, and fear crested. Fear that if she wasn't careful she'd convince herself to stay, to settle for being a mere convenient wife rather than someone he cherished.

'It's not up to you to *let* me go anywhere.' Emma took refuge in anger, though it was only surface deep. She was too miserable to muster real outrage.

Then he did what she'd feared. Instead of blustering he turned gentle. As if he really cared about her.

'I'm worried about you, *glyka mou*. What's happened?'

Emma drew a slow breath and raised her eyes to his. 'I can't go on like this. I can't—' she waved one hand in the air '—keep up the pretence for a whole twelve months. This isn't going to work.'

From concerned, his proud features immediately turned stony. 'How can you say that? It's working beautifully.'

She shook her head, tugging her gaze away, feeling the instant ease in tension as she did. 'For you. For Anthea maybe. But not for me. I just can't do it any more.'

Emma registered a ripple of movement in his big frame, as if from a rising tide of energy. 'But you will. You gave your word.'

His voice was cooler than she'd heard in ages, each word clipped. The voice of a stranger.

'No! You forced me into a situation where I had no choice. I took your devil's bargain because that's all I could do. But it's impossible.'

Christo stepped towards her and she shrank back. Instantly he froze.

'Please.' Her voice wobbled and she had to work to get the words out. 'I need to be alone.'

Emma's breath came in laboured gasps. She swung around and fumbled for her sandals. But as she scrambled towards the path a hard hand closed around her elbow.

'Not so fast.'

CHAPTER FOURTEEN

CHRISTO REELED. HALF an hour ago they'd been wrapped in each other, lost in a blast of ecstasy so intense he was sure it had marked him for life.

Emma had marked him. Her sweet generosity. Her fiery strength. Her gentle caring.

He'd never known a woman like her. Had never expected to and had certainly never anticipated the effect she'd have on him.

Now he was entangled, caught so fast in the net of his own longing that there was no escape.

She couldn't expect him to let her go. Not now. Not when he'd glimpsed paradise with her. Christo had learned never to expect miracles. Everything in his world always came at a price.

But, despite everything, Emma had given herself to him freely, unstintingly. Not just in bed, but in so many other ways, ways that made him think the boundaries he'd known all his life could be broken. That if he made the effort perhaps there could be *more*.

He wanted that more so badly. He wanted Emma.

'Talk to me, Emma.' Nausea stirred at the thought of her so distressed. Of *him* distressing her. She trembled in his hold but didn't try to escape.

'What is it? Is it because of what I did? Because I didn't save Cassie?' Before he'd shared that, Emma had been content in his arms.

Guilt over his stepsister lay heavily, only lightening occasionally. When Anthea smiled her increasingly cheeky grin or put her hand in his. Or when Emma gave him that glowing look that made his heart stop.

'What?' Emma turned and his gut contracted when he saw that her lashes were spiked with tears.

'You despise me, don't you?' The words ground from him, revealing the depths of his fear.

Once he'd never have admitted that to anyone, even himself. He'd learned, almost before he could walk, to conceal weakness. But Emma stripped away his ability to pretend. Self-preservation should have kept his mouth shut about the past, but for once he'd wanted to share everything because it was Emma wanting to know.

Look where that had got him.

'I don't despise you.' Her words were choked and unconvincing.

Christo's pulse beat raggedly. He knew he'd guessed right. Yet still he couldn't release her. He slid his hand to her wrist, feeling the tumultuous pulse there.

'Then what? You weren't in a hurry to leave before I told you about Cassie.'

'It's not that.' Her gaze slid from his and Christo felt the lie like a blow to the back of his legs severing his tendons.

Now he found the willpower to release her and step back.

'Don't lie to me, Emma.' That was one of the things he treasured about her. She always told him the truth.

'I'm not—' He felt her gaze on him. 'Christo? Are you all right?'

He grimaced. Even now, when she knew the worst of his faults, Emma could find it in her to be concerned for him. She was too caring for her own good.

'No. I'm not.' He hefted a breath, trying to fill lungs that had seized. Looking down into drenched hazel eyes Christo realised he had no option but to tell *her* the truth. The whole truth, that he'd been grappling with for weeks now. 'I can't let you go.'

She stepped back and Christo felt as if he'd cracked right through the middle, seeing her retreat.

'You have to.' He heard her desperation and knew this was his last chance.

Pride be damned. He couldn't let her go without a fight. 'I need you, Emma. Please. I...love you.'

He'd never thought to hear, much less say, those words. They were foreign on his tongue but as soon as he said them something that felt remarkably like peace settled around him.

It was short-lived.

Emma flung up her hand as if to ward him off. 'Don't, please. That's too cruel.'

Gently Christo captured her hand and pulled it down, resisting the impulse to tug her to him and never let her go. 'Why is it cruel?'

He was the one being rejected. But seeing Emma so distraught tempered his reaction.

Sad brown eyes met his. 'You're just saying that because you know that I...' Her chin came up. 'I was in love with you when we married. You think you can make me stay if you pretend to love me now.'

Christo shook his head, ignoring the dart of pain at the fact she spoke of loving him in the past tense.

'I'm not pretending, *karthia mou*. I promised to be honest with you.' He paused, watching her eyes widen. 'I want more than a convenient marriage. I want you as my partner, my love, the one that I cherish for the rest of my days.'

Instead of the response he'd hoped for, Emma's mouth turned down at the corners. Pain clouded her expression.

'It's too late, Christo. Once I might have fallen for that, but not now.'

'I see. You don't trust me after all.' He couldn't blame her. He'd set about winning her with ruthless efficiency. Now, looking back on his determination to put his ring on Emma's finger, he understood it was because he'd been falling for her from the very first. At the time he hadn't had the emotional understanding to recognise he was falling in love, yet he'd known instinctively he needed this woman in his life.

Emma shook her head, her hair a tangle around her shoulders. Her red top was inside out, her skirt drooping on one side where the zip hadn't pulled up all the way, and her nose was pink. She was still the most beautiful woman he knew. Christo's heart gave a mighty thud, as if trying to leap free of his rib cage and throw itself on her mercy.

'I won't hold you to our agreement.' It killed him to say it but how could he keep her by force? 'Your uncle's business is safe. Your assets are too.'

He read surprise on her face and pushed harder.

'That's what I was going to tell you today. That I want this to be a real marriage. That I want more from you than just a legal agreement and a home for Anthea.'

Her chin tilted. 'And sex.'

He nodded. 'And sex.' The thought had an inevitable effect with a surge of blood to the groin. 'I want more, Emma. I'm greedy. I want *you*. The whole of you. I want to be the one you care for because I care for you. I *love* you.' The words came easier this time, despite the fact he felt stretched on a torture rack by her lack of response.

Christo stood, waiting for her to capitulate, to admit she cared for him even a little. To give him hope.

Nothing. Just that frozen look of shock.

Defeat was a boulder crushing his chest, flattening his very being. Yet he couldn't give up. His feelings for her were too vital.

Finally he dragged out the words. 'I won't stand in your way, Emma. But, wherever you go, I'll be there. Hoping you change your mind. If you go to Melbourne, I'll buy a home there. If you stay in the Corfu villa, I'll look for a place nearby.' He dragged his hand through his hair, silently admitting his desperation. 'After all, you'll want to see Anthea from time to time.' He prayed she did. It looked like being the only way he'd get to see Emma.

'But your business is based in Athens!'

Christo huffed out a terse laugh. 'You think that will stop me?' He shook his head. 'For you I'd give that up. I've got more than enough money for a lifetime.' As he said it Christo felt an unexpected sense of freedom. Never in his life had he contemplated a world without Karides Enterprises. 'There's more to life than business.'

His father would be spinning in his grave.

But this was his life. Not his father's.

Emma faltered back a step, her hand going to her throat. 'You couldn't. It's your life.'

'*Part* of my life,' he said slowly. 'A part that I enjoy, most of the time. But there are more important things in my life now. Like you.'

Emma heard his words and told herself this was a trap to keep her in a convenient marriage.

But when she saw the excitement and wonder in Christo's eyes it was hard not to believe him.

'I'm not my father, Emma. I saw his life and I didn't want it, even as I spent my time learning how to be him.'

'No,' she whispered, unable to stop herself. 'You aren't him. He sent Cassie away. You tried to help her. You're helping her daughter.'

That had to count for something. Christo was a better man than his father.

'I love you, *karthia mou*.' There were those words again. He called her 'his heart'. How was a woman supposed to resist that? 'Ah, Emma, don't cry.' He lifted a finger to her face, brushing away the single tear that had spilled down her cheek. 'I didn't mean to hurt you.'

'I just don't know what to believe.'

His hand dropped. 'If nothing else, believe I'll never intentionally hurt you again.' Christo swallowed. 'I've got a lot to learn, like how to care for a family. Maybe that's why I was so determined to win you and keep you. For my own selfish reasons and not for Anthea at all. I understood, though I couldn't admit it, that I needed you. For your beautiful, loving heart.'

To Emma's amazement he took a step away. A chill enveloped her.

'If I thought it would work I'd promise you jewels and designer clothes. There's a luxury yacht off Santorini, a ski chalet at St Moritz and a chateau in the Loire.' As she watched, his intent gaze grew cloudy. 'But I know you, Emma. You care about people more than things. There's nothing more I can say. Words alone won't convince you.'

His eyes were bleak, his sensual mouth a grim line. Every line of that strong, superb body spoke of pain.

And it struck her that she believed him. These weren't empty words. He really would change his life to win her, move to Australia to be with her.

Even in the days of their courtship Christo hadn't actively lied. She'd been the one spinning fairy tales out of his kindness and gentle wooing, building them into far more than he'd ever implied.

She stared into those smoky eyes, feeling the depth of pain he didn't bother to conceal. Christo stood there, uncaring about his nakedness, as if nothing mattered but convincing her.

'You'd really give up the business for me?'

Fire sparked in those eyes. Emma saw blue flames ignite. 'I'll do whatever it takes. Just say the word.'

Abruptly the dreadful tightness wrapping her ribs eased and she took a shuddery breath of relief. Of hope.

'I might still want those designer clothes if I'm going to look like a billionaire's woman.'

The fire in his eyes became a blaze of heat as he absorbed her words. 'Clothes don't make the woman, Emma.'

'Or the man.' She nodded at his naked body and he shrugged, a smile flickering at the corner of his mouth.

'I'm hoping you'll decide it's what's inside that counts.'

If Emma hadn't been so close she'd never have seen the shadow of self-doubt in his expression. Never have noticed the way his pulse thundered too hard at his temple. As if, despite all his experience bringing off hugely profitable deals, Christo still feared he wasn't good enough for her.

Emma stepped up to him, putting her hand to his pounding chest. 'There's something you should know.'

Christo's hand clamped hers to him. His jaw tightened, as if expecting the worst. 'Tell me.'

'I tried but I never fell out of love with you.'

It took long seconds for her words to sink in. 'You still love me?' Beneath her hand Christo's heart took up a helter-skelter rhythm that matched hers.

Emma nodded and suddenly they were both grinning. His hands framed her face. 'You love me.' This time he said it as if he believed it.

'And you love me.' Now she could see it in his face, feel it in the rippling tremor that passed through him. How wrong she'd been, imagining Christo incapable of deep emotion. For there it was, clear as day.

Then his hands were on her, not undressing her or seducing her, but lifting her high and swirling her round and round till the world spun and the only solid thing in it was Christo.

Finally he stopped, panting, and collapsed on the sand, cushioning her as she landed on him.

'My own Emma.' He wrapped his arms around her. 'You give me heart to be the man I never thought I could be.'

'And you give me courage to be more than I'd ever thought possible.' The moment felt so huge, so momentous.

'Stop talking and kiss me, wife.'

Instead of taking offence at his command, Emma gladly complied. Then she made a demand of her own, which provoked one of Christo's trademark sexy smiles and kept them on the beach for hours celebrating.

EPILOGUE

AFTER MONTHS OF detailed planning and intense work the neighbouring villa was finally open. The residence was elegant and well-appointed and the gardens a triumph. Christo's staff had provided expert assistance but it was Emma and her team of locals who'd pulled it all together.

Christo stood in the sunken garden, redolent with the velvet scent of roses, cypresses and the salt tang of the sea. The days grew shorter but, as if ordained by fate, or perhaps his wife's sheer positivity, the afternoon sun shone bright in a cloudless sky.

His gaze wandered from the draperies of sea-green gauze and silk that led from the shallow steps, past the flowering shrubs, to the pergola where he stood. The place had a festive air.

'You look like the cat who swallowed the cream.'

Christo turned to Damen, grinning beside him.

'Can you blame me?'

His friend shook his head. 'The transformation is stunning.'

Christo knew he was talking about the villa, once sad and neglected, now an inviting showpiece. But the real change, he knew, was within himself. He was a different man from the one who'd flown to Melbourne to secure a commercial property and a convenient wife.

Not for the first time he paused to wonder at old man Katsoyiannis agreeing to the deal. He'd been as sharp as a tack, nobody's fool, and so protective of his granddaughter. Had he seen what Christo hadn't? That Emma was the perfect woman for him?

'Emma's the one responsible.' Not just for the renovation, but for the change in him.

'She's a miracle worker, and not only with bricks and mortar.' Damen clapped him on the shoulder. 'I've never seen you looking so relaxed, or so happy.'

Christo shrugged, not bothering to conceal a smile. 'What can I say? Marriage agrees with me.' It wasn't just the fact that he delegated more and worked mainly from their home in Corfu. The life he shared with Emma and little Anthea was filled with joy. 'You should try it.'

Ignoring Damen's choke of shock, he turned away.

There was Dora, surrounded by relatives and friends. The familiar faces he'd come to know from Corfu. A scattering of invitees from Athens. On the other side of the garden Emma's cousin Maia chatted to Clio, both looking effortlessly chic, and both ignoring the attempts of men aged from seventeen to seventy to catch their attention.

Neither woman could hold a candle to his Emma.

'There she is.' Damen's voice made him look past the crowd.

At first all he saw was Emma's friend Steph descending the steps to the garden. Did that explain the breathless quality of Damen's voice? Christo hadn't missed the undercurrent between them.

Then he forgot all else as he caught sight of Emma.

Once again she wore the slim-fitting gown of cream that made her waist look impossibly small and she as fragile as gossamer.

Except his wife was anything but fragile. She was strong and determined, but kind and caring too. *Loving.*

His breath escaped on the thought.

Loving. That was Emma.

Her head was up, an antique lace veil framing her features. With every step the tourmaline eardrops he'd given her swung and gleamed, but they couldn't outshine the happiness on her face. As Emma's eyes met his Christo felt that familiar thump, as if their two hearts beat as one. Then she smiled and the world turned radiant.

Her uncle walked beside her, beaming. And…

'Cwisto!' Anthea barrelled into his legs, wrapping her arms around his thighs and crushing her posy of flowers.

'Here, sweetie, stand with me.' Steph, in her green bridesmaid's dress, beckoned the little girl, but Anthea shook her head.

'Can't I stay with you, Cwisto?' Big brown eyes met his. He knew he was being manipulated but did he care?

'Of course.' He took her hand in his. 'You're part of this too.'

For, in renewing their vows, Emma committed herself to both of them. As he committed himself to her.

Then Emma's uncle led her forward and Christo took his bride's hand, drawing her close. Never had he felt such profound emotion as when he saw the love in her clear gaze.

'You take my breath away, *karthia mou.*' He bent his head and gathered her to him, kissing her until he felt her turn satisfyingly boneless.

A small hand tugged his trouser leg and Anthea's piercing whisper penetrated. 'Not *now*, Cwisto. Be good. You have to wait till *after* the pwomises.'

The crowd laughed and Emma's eyes danced as she leaned back, breathless, in his embrace. 'Yes, there's plenty of time for kisses later.'

'I'll hold you to that, *agapi mou.*' Then, grinning, he lifted Anthea in his other arm and turned to the celebrant.

* * * * *

MILLS & BOON

Coming next month

A SCANDALOUS MIDNIGHT IN MADRID
Susan Stephens

Sadie had never seen a live flamenco show, let alone visited an encampment in the mountains devoted to the art. She didn't know what to expect and was excited. Alejandro had explained as they set out on horseback that professional artistes came from all over the world to study at the camp so they could hone their craft and pass on the artistry.

The steep mountain track finally opened onto a wider trail that led in turn to a surprising plateau that housed what she could only describe as a hidden city in the mountains, where gaily painted caravans had replaced the more traditional snow-white houses in the village. Deep caves were carved into a menacing rock face at one side of this heavily populated carpet of green, while craggy, snow-capped peaks clawed at the sky above them, but what surprised Sadie most of all was how warm it was.

'The flamenco camp enjoys a micro climate,' Alejandro explained when she asked the question, 'which was why it was set up here.'

The hidden city was a bustling place, and their arrival caused a great deal of excitement. The Gypsy King had returned from his travels, Sadie concluded as crowds began to mass along the way. She could see now where Alejandro got his good looks. The dark flashing eyes and glossy black hair of his people was unmistakable. He was one of them, imperious and proud with incredible bone structure. He had the same hawkish stare, chiselled features, and stern, authoritative air. A group of men came forward to lead his horse into camp, and they talked in a language she didn't recognise. Alejandro slipped easily into this new, exotic tongue. A Spanish duke, who was equally at home in the mountains as in the salons of Madrid, with a gypsy princess mother, and an aristocratic father. How could his history be any more fascinating? She almost preferred this rougher, far more dangerous-looking man, than the polished Don, who all but ruled in Madrid. The downside was that she felt like a mouse in her jeans and nondescript top. If she'd known there would be such a welcome—she'd still be wearing jeans and a nondescript top. This welcome was for Alejandro, a man who made her senses riot.

Tensing, she held her breath as Alejandro insisted on lifting her down from the horse. In those few seconds, she was aware of everything about him: his heat, his potency, his outrageous good looks, and the warm clean man smell he exuded.

'Would you like to dance?' he asked, noticing her staring at the stage.

'Like this?' She grimaced as she stared down at her workman-like clothes.

'Why not?' He flashed a look that seared her from the inside out.

'Better not. I'll only tread on your toes.'

'What I meant,' he explained, 'was, would you like to take a flamenco class?'

He really was the expert in making her cheeks blaze red. 'I have two left feet, and no sense of rhythm,' she said, recovering fast.

'Have you ever put that to the test?'

The expression in Alejandro's eyes made his simple enquiry sound like the most dangerous suggestion. Her imagination working overtime again, Sadie concluded. 'Okay,' she said in the spirit of keeping things cool between them. 'I'll have a go.'

'Would you like some help?' Alejandro asked with the faintest of smiles.

Continue reading
A SCANDALOUS MIDNIGHT IN MADRID
Susan Stephens

Available next month
www.millsandboon.co.uk